A COWBOY'S WORD

I stepped over to the counter, and when the woman looked up from her ledger I tipped my hat to her. Her eyes were as dark as her hair. They were pretty eyes, and bright, but they had a certain sadness behind them, too.

I reached inside my coat and brought out the letter I'd written the night before. "I'd like to mail this. It's to the folks. I don't know if they will write to me or not," I said. "My name's Casey Wills and I'm livin' at Trujillo Camp across the line on the XIT."

"Why wouldn't they write, Mr. Wills?"

"It's been a long time. I don't even know but what they might be dead—maybe for years."

"Well, Mr. Wills, my name is Lillie Johnson, and if you get any mail I will hold it for you."

"I'd be much obliged," I said.

"That'll be two cents . . . postage on your letter."

I smiled, embarrassed. "Sorry, ma'am, but right now I don't have it. I could wait till payday to mail it, but I kinda wanted it to get there by Christmas. . . . If you could give me credit I'll sure be good for it."

"I'll pay the postage on it myself, Mr. Wills. I'll take your word that you will come back and pay me."

"You can count on it," I promised. . . .

───────────────

"This western by a poet and . . . cowboy is a real treat for readers who enjoy words and people. Very good reading, even re-reading."

— *Library Journal*

PRAISE FOR SAM BROWN'S PREVIOUS NOVELS

THE CRIME OF COY BELL

"Carefully plotted, with fully-realized characters, this novel has a double-clutch surprise ending both believable and thought-provoking. The best Western novel of this young year."

—*Booklist*

"A new novel by Texas panhandle writer Sam Brown, *The Crime of Coy Bell* [is] about a cowboy who makes the grave mistake of falling in love with his boss' wife. Brown, a working cowboy, is author of two other novels, both excellent, *The Long Season* and *The Trail to Honk Ballard's Bones*."

—Dale L. Walker, *Rocky Mountain News*

THE TRAIL TO HONK BALLARD'S BONES

"A page-turner, strong on characterization, plot and background. . . . The characterization of the woman, incidentally, is one of the strengths that put this novel far above the quality of the average Western and in a whole different world from the one created by the founders of the genre. . . . Brown has honed his skills to a new sharpness. . . . It's a case of good writing and good reading, recommended not only for Western fans but for any reader who enjoys a good story well told."

—*Amarillo Sunday News-Globe*

Books by Sam Brown

The Crime of Coy Bell
The Trail to Honk Ballard's Bones
The Long Season
The Big Lonely

SAM BROWN

The Big Lonely

POCKET BOOKS

New York London Toronto Sydney Tokyo Singapore

This book is a work of fiction. Names, characters, places and incidents either are products of the author's imagination or are used fictitiously. Any resemblance to actual events or locales or persons, living or dead, is entirely coincidental.

POCKET BOOKS, a division of Simon & Schuster Inc.
1230 Avenue of the Americas, New York, NY 10020

Copyright © 1992 by Sam Brown

Published by arrangement with Walker and Company

ISBN: 0-671-86547-1

First Pocket Books printing May 1994

10 9 8 7 6 5 4 3 2 1

POCKET and colophon are registered trademarks of Simon & Schuster Inc.

Cover art by Tim Tanner

Printed in the U.S.A.

**The
Big
Lonely**

CHAPTER
1

We'd been at it a long time, forever it seemed like, and we'd gathered a huge scope of country. We'd started out in summer—the summer of 1887—under a sun that could draw sweat from a horse who was doing nothing other than switching his tail at flies. And we'd started out far to the south, up on the flats, where there are no trees or brush, clear to the end of the world; where the country is so flat that if it ever rains the water can't decide which way it is to the sea, and, even if it could decide, it couldn't find any means to get there. No rivers or creeks cut across that tabletop country, just a wide-bottomed draw here and there that goes nowhere. So when it rains, the water wanders with not much more sense of direction than a blind cow with the staggers until finally enough of it gathers at the end of one of those little draws that go nowhere to make a little poor excuse of a lake. In a few days all the water that collected there during the rain is gone, having given itself up to the sun and the wind, leaving nothing to mark where it had been except a patch of brown earth that soon cracks and curls under the sun and is scattered, a speck of dust at a time, by the ceaseless wind.

After several weeks up on the flats, making big circles and gathering cattle, moving the wagon mostly east and west but with always a slightly northward slant to the moves, it was a true relief when finally, sometime near first frost, we reached the edge of the breaks. Here there were a few mesquites, and the same sort of draws that went nowhere up on the flats now sometimes led to a sandy, narrow creek bed that, while usually dry, had scattered thickets of wild plums and even an occasional cottonwood tree along it.

That little sandy creek, winding between gently sloping, sage-covered hills, would usually lead to a bigger creek, and that one would lead to another still bigger, until finally there would be a creek big enough to have sliced down through the earth and made a narrow canyon where small springs fed the creek and where cottonwoods and even cedars and grape bushes grew like they meant to stay. The canyon walls would be steep and rocky, and on top of the walls would be a rimrock where a cow pony could only get off in a few places and then only if he really tended to business.

This kind of country, while not as monotonous to a cowboy and usually more agreeable with his disposition than an open country is, is nonetheless harder to gather cattle out of and more dangerous, too. Both the flat, treeless, endless expanse of the llano and the canyons and rimrocks of the breaks take a lot out of a man.

The weather takes its toll on a man, too. You start out in a deep fry and finish up in a deep freeze. You start out sweating on top of your bedroll at night, and before the wagon pulls in you'll be pulling your tarp up over your head, trying to sleep through a cold rain, or maybe when you throw the tarp back some morning you'll also be throwing back a couple of inches of fresh snow.

But the work goes on and on . . . and on. The wagon sets up somewhere, and just as you get used to the landscape in your new yard, the fly is jerked down, you throw your bedroll in the hoodlum wagon and move to a new place with a new yard and all new fixtures. You move maybe ten, twenty or thirty times, and then you lose count.

You get wrung out and used up, and then one night the wagon boss says, "Boys, tomorrow oughta wind 'er up and get us laid by for winter."

So now the works were finished and we were trailing the remuda of horses into Alamocitas Camp, which at that time was not only the headquarters of that division of the XIT but the general headquarters for the entire outfit.

Every cowboy in the outfit had his coat collar turned up and buttoned over his neckerchief. Scattered dry pellets of snow came in on a bitter wind from the north, from somewhere across the Canadian River. My left ear ached because of the cold, and it was painful to wiggle the stiff toes inside my boots.

There were a dozen cowboys bringing in the horses, including myself—Casey Wills. The remuda was strung out, two or three abreast and giving no trouble, following the chuck wagon and the hoodlum wagon. In fact, they would have followed the chuck wagon into the home ranch, as many of us called Alamocitas Camp: we weren't driving them so much as we were just going along with them. And we weren't talking much, just listening to the sounds of the horses and the jingle and creak of saddles, bridles and spurs.

I think most cowboys feel quieter when they're trailing the remuda into the home ranch after fall works than they do at almost any other time. It's not that you're not glad the works is finally over or that you don't have some feeling of accomplishment. And when you've been sleeping on the ground every night for several months straight, the thought of a real bed, soft and warm, is appealing. And you look forward to relaxing in a tub of hot water until all the dust and grime soak off and float to the top in a thick scum. You know how good clean clothes will feel, and you know you can—and probably will—stay up all night drinking whiskey, and come the next crack of dawn, you'll still be in bed instead of forked over the back of some remuda horse.

And of course you think of women. You know most of them are far more treacherous than most of the horses you've been on, but they smell different and they're softer, too.

But even though all of that is true, there is a sort of melancholy feeling that usually follows a bunch of cowboys back to the home ranch, just as the cowboys follow the remuda and the remuda follows the chuck wagon, all of them moving slow.

I'm not sure what it is that causes the quietness and the melancholy. Maybe part of it is the shortening of the days and chilling of the weather. Winter's coming on, and there's nothing you can do about it. And maybe part of it is the feeling that something has ended that never will be again, for each works, even on the same outfit, is different. And you're tired, too, just like the horses are. Both of you were snorty and full of play when the works began; now both are gentle and a little gaunt looking.

When you're dragging into the home ranch in the fall, you also get to thinking. You think of things that have happened during that particular works, and then you start to remember other works in other places. You remember places you've been and sights you've seen. Sometimes you might feel a shiver, and it's nothing to do with the weather. Maybe as you look at the dust rising into the air behind the horses, a sudden picture comes into your mind of a time some puncher you knew got tangled to his horse and you couldn't reach him in time.

Or maybe you recall the time when you were a youngster living at home with the folks and thinking you would *never* grow up. . . . Maybe you remember some childhood sweetheart and how you thought life was going to be then—and how different it all turned out.

I watched as the wagons topped a rise and then disappeared over it and the lead horses trailing just behind them disappeared, too, and then the horses just behind the leaders disappeared in the same way, all walking weary. Then I looked at the back of the cowboy riding in front of me—Josh Smith. I thought back to the first time I saw him, several years ago on another outfit, and remembered how strong and agile he had been then; now he was so stove up he had trouble getting on a horse. At one time he'd handled a rope prettier and with more ease than anyone I'd known, but now his shoulder was so stiff and sore he could hardly swing a loop at all. The years and the wrecks on countless cow outfits had taken their toll on Josh.

I lifted my own right arm, I guess out of reflex, and wondered if the stiffness in the shoulder when I got my elbow up past shoulder level was due to the cold or my imagination—or the years and the wrecks on countless cow outfits.

Then I had a thought that I had just as soon not had, but maybe it's the feeling that's really behind the mysterious draggin'-to-the-home-ranch-in-the-fall melancholy: in a lot of ways the fall works on an outfit is patterned like a cowboy's life shrunk into a few short months—you start out with a step and a swing that's free and strong . . . and you finish up tired and slow.

Alamocitas Camp was in rolling-hills and sagebrush country, and we could see the camp to the east of us several miles before we got there. Once there we would have to pull the shoes off the horses that would be turned out on grass that winter and not caught again until spring. But then we would be free to catch fresh horses and trot to Tascosa.

As we pushed the remuda into the big set of pens at Alamocitas, I started wondering if a certain girl was still in Tascosa, and I hoped she was. Her name was Florence, and the last time I had been in Tascosa she was at the Edward's Hotel and Saloon. She was sort of gaunt then, and I was hoping she'd been on better feed and had put on a little flesh since I'd seen her.

An hour after getting to Alamocitas we had the shoes pulled off all the grass horses. Most of the boys were in the bunkhouse, where it was warm, but for some reason me and Ab Deacons, Johnnie Lester and Josh Smith were squatted on the south side of the saddle house, out of the wind, thumping pebbles at some old hens who didn't have any more sense than we did—they could have been in the henhouse but instead were scratching in the loose dirt and dried horse manure that had piled up around the edges of the corral. Neither of us, chickens or cowboys, were making much noise, just scratching or thumping in the cold.

In his late twenties, Ab Deacons was the youngest of the four of us. He was six feet tall and quiet, with sandy hair and blue eyes. I'd never seen him before the wagon pulled out and didn't know anything about him, except that he was a good cowboy with a Dixie heritage—what more does any man need to know about another?

Me and Johnnie Lester were about the same age and height—late thirties and an inch or so short of six feet. We were both straight and slim, of course, as most men who live in the saddle and sleep on the ground are. Johnnie had darker hair than I did, and he had a heavy mustache while I had none. He also had a bad scar on his right cheek where a horse kicked him one time. Johnnie was a good cowboy, too, damn good. I'd known him for a long time, and if he ever once had a serious thought in his life, he never let it show.

I'd known Josh Smith forever. He was the oldest of us. I don't know for sure just how old, but somewhere in his late fifties. His onetime coal black hair was now salt and pepper with more salt than pepper. He was six-two and weighed about two hundred. When I first saw him he probably wouldn't have weighed over one eighty, but the years had spread him out a bit and had even given him a little belly—along with stiffened joints and a slower swing. Josh's way had always been the "goddammit to hell!" way. He had lived like his body was a battering ram that he could use to beat life into submission. He could be dangerous to his friends and disastrous to his enemies, but I liked Josh. If it was proper I would even admit to loving the old devil, but it's not proper, so I'll not admit it.

A little time passed quietly by, and I started thinking of home again and my folks and wondering if they were dead or alive and of all the years that lay between me and them. Then for some reason I thought of a man I helped hang in Wyoming for stealing horses and how he said he wished he could see his mother one more time. I was thinking of some other things, too, and all of them things a stray dog of a cowboy shouldn't think about, not after it's too late to do anything about any of them.

Finally, Josh broke the silence and asked, "Reckon they'll let us winter on this outfit or are we gonna have to ride the grub line till spring?"

"Guess we'll have to ask Billy," Ab said. Billy Nye was wagon boss of that division of the XIT.

"Here he comes now," Josh said, looking toward the bunkhouse. "Or at least here comes somebody."

"That's that goddamn Findlay feller from Shi-caw-go," Johnnie said.

Findlay was as foreign to us as if he'd been from the moon. He talked and dressed like an easterner and sat a horse like a two-by-four. He had been hanging around our wagon for a week or so confabbing with Billy Nye and taking notes of some kind. He acted like it galled the hell out of him to even have to speak to anybody lower on the totem pole than a wagon boss.

Findlay walked on up to where we were and announced, "I'm going to saddle a mount and check on the range conditions over in the Torrey's Peak vicinity."

Before any of us could say how fine we thought it was that he was going to do such a thing, Findlay asked, "Now that this cattle working period is over with, men, what will you be doing next?"

"I reckon we'll be goin' to Tascosa to get bathed, bred, blind and broke," Ab said without batting an eye but looking serious at Findlay.

"But you'll be back on the job tomorrow, I suppose," Findlay said in a Chicago sort of way.

Johnnie looked up at Findlay and stretched his mustache into a wide grin. "By this time tomorrow, Mr. Findlay, we'll have been bathed and bred but we'll still be in the midst of bein' blind and we won't be hardly broke yet. I guess these things take more time in Texas than they do in Chicago, but we just keep hangin' in till we get 'er done."

"Well," Findlay said, "I suppose that's fine if Mr. Nye terminates your employment this afternoon but—"

"I suppose that's a *fact,* whether Mr. Nye terminates the whole goddamn world today or not, Mr. Findlay," Johnnie said.

"But surely you don't expect you could remain on the company payroll and—"

"We've *got* to, Mr. Findlay," Ab said. "It's the law."

"The law?" Findlay said, reaching inside his coat pocket for his notebook. "And who made this . . . this law?"

Ab looked down at the fistful of pebbles in his hand and then said, "I'm not sure whether it was U. S. Grant or whether it was old High-Chin Bob from the Brazos. . . . Who do you think it was, Casey?"

"Moses," I said.

"I see," Findlay said as he put his notebook back in his pocket without writing on it and walked on into the saddle house, drug out his saddle and saddled a horse.

As Findlay was riding away Josh glanced up from the cigarette he was rolling and said dryly, "He cuts a helluva figure on a horse, don't he?"

CHAPTER
2

Findlay was just riding out of camp when Billy Nye stepped out of the bunkhouse. Billy watched Findlay for a few seconds and then came on over to the saddle house.

"Where's he goin'?" Billy asked.

"He's goin' over around Torrey's Peak to check on the 'range conditions,'" Ab said. "I wonder what he's got in mind to do if they don't suit him?"

"Well," Billy said, "being as how he's the bookkeeper on this outfit, maybe if they don't suit him he'll order us up a nice rain or a wet snow."

"I wonder how they'll get it here from Shi-caw-go?" Johnnie said out of the side of his mouth.

"Just what's he doin' here anyway?" I asked. "Chicago is a long ways to come just to check 'range conditions.' Looks like it would have been simpler to've written a letter and asked you."

"He didn't come out here just to check the grass," Billy said. "He came to spy on us."

11

We all exchanged quick glances. *"Spy* on us?" Johnnie said. "What 'n the hell for?"

"Don't know for sure," Billy answered. "All I know is what I've heard on the wind, and that is that the big segundos in Chicago don't like the way Campbell is runnin' things out here. They think we're losin' too many cattle to the long-loops."

Old "Barbecue" Campbell was the general manager of the whole outfit. Josh was the only one of us who knew Campbell. This fall works was the first time me or Johnnie or Ab had ever worked for the XIT, but Josh had been with them for two years, the longest he'd ever stayed with one outfit. He said Campbell was "mouthy and arrogant" but that he left the cowboys alone. The only time the rest of us had seen him was about two weeks earlier, when he came to the wagon to introduce Findlay to Billy.

The "long-loops" Billy said the segundos in Chicago were worried about were cowboys who had a bad habit of throwing their loops a little farther than they had intended and drawing it up around the wrong beef, all by intentional mistake of course.

"Findlay's not the only one spyin', either," Billy went on. "There's another feller nosin' around, too, a man named Matlock, a lawyer from south Texas. I ain't seen him yet, but I know him—and I know he don't have any use for me."

"Why's that, Billy?" Ab asked.

"Well, at one time Matlock was one of them prosecutin' attorney type of fellers down at Vernon, where I was draggin' my shadow around. I got a little too popular with the local citizenry for my own good, and one day they all got together and invited me to a hangin', which sounded like a lot of fun until I found out it was my own hangin' they had in mind to celebrate. Matlock talked them into withdrawin' that invitation on the condition that I'd promise to leave and not come back unless I floated in on the ark during the second flood. I made that promise pretty damned quick and I've kept 'er too, but I understand Matlock turned a little red faced when he learned I was a wagon boss here."

It didn't come as any great shock to us that our wagon boss, the man we took orders from, had barely escaped a hanging somewhere else, and we didn't figure it was our place to pry into the particulars of the matter because it wasn't any of our business, just like we figured our own pasts weren't anybody's business but ours.

"I've been noticin' that bulge in your coat pocket, Billy," Johnnie said.

Billy smiled again as he pulled out a bottle of Yellow Rose whiskey, or what was left of it, and said, "Oh yeah, I was bringing this out to you. The boys in the bunkhouse passed it around already. There's not much more than a drink apiece left, but you're welcome to it." Then he handed the bottle to Johnnie.

"Findlay told me just this morning that it looked to him like the ranch was harborin' a bunch of drunks, bums and thieves," Billy said, while we were passing around the bottle.

"What!" Josh said, holding the bottle of Yellow Rose poised to take his drink. He lowered the bottle and said to Ab, "Throw me the makin's."

"What'd you do with that last sack you stole out of my bedroll?" Ab replied.

"Why what 'n the hell do you mean, Ab?" he said. "I smoked the damn stuff, whadaya think I did with it?"

"Soon as we get to town, Josh," Ab said, "me an' you are goin' to a store and you're buyin' *both* of us some tobacco—that is, *if* the eagle's landed."

Billy took Ab's hint, reaching inside his coat and saying, "She's landed, boys—I got your pay right here. . . . I guess when you were talkin' to Findlay you did everything you could to throw as bad a light as possible on the outfit?"

"Why no!" Johnnie said, and then, "Oh, I think we did say something about going to town for a couple of days—but just long enough to go to prayer meetin' and pay our tithes."

We had four months' wages coming, which made us wealthy men, considering the fact that we were drawing twenty-five dollars a month. But out of my nest egg, I owed Billy for some tobacco I'd gotten from him and I owed three men in the bunkhouse some money I'd lost playing cards at night around the wagon. By the time I'd paid everybody I owed, I had sixty-six dollars left. It felt good having money again, and I was determined, although I knew it would be against customary cowboy behavior, to not put all of it in circulation in town as soon as I could. As a matter of fact, I was determined to *leave* town with money in my pocket.

"We gonna get to winter here?" Johnnie asked as Billy started walking back toward the bunkhouse.

Billy stopped and turned back and said, "I don't know yet, boys. Don't know how many men the higher-ups are gonna let me keep on. I'll find out later on this afternoon though. Why don't I meet y'all tonight at about eight o'clock in the Exchange Saloon, and I'll buy you a drink and let you know then."

"Let's rattle our hocks to town, boys," Johnnie said. If he had ever felt the melancholy, having money in his hand and a trip to town in his immediate future was enough to cure him.

As we were dragging our saddles out of the saddle house and laying them in the dirt in the corral, Josh said, "What in the hell are you being so quiet about, Casey?"

"Didn't know I was" was my response, but of course I did know I was—I just didn't know exactly why. Although I knew I was going to town, I didn't really want to go. What I really wanted to do was to catch a horse and ride to a rim above the river and just sit there alone and watch the red waters of the Canadian roll by. But I had faith that feeling would pass in time. It always had before.

Instead of company horses it was personal horses that we roped and led out of the bunch in the corral and threw our saddles on. We hoped we'd get to stay on through the winter, but right then we weren't on the company payroll. Besides, it was a twenty- or twenty-five-mile trot to Tascosa, and we wanted fresh horses to make that trot on, and since our personal horses had been turned out in a little grass trap at Alamocitas all fall they were sure enough fresh. They might have been a little too fat and soft, but they weren't used up and wore out like all the company horses we'd just brought in behind the wagon were.

I had two horses of my own, a gray and a bay, and it was the gray that I roped, saddled and got on.

"God," Johnnie said as he got on his horse, "I hope that Raven is still in Tascosa! I've been thinkin' about her ever' night for two months. The last time I saw her was over a year ago at the Cattleman Saloon. . . . God, I hope she's still there!"

"Didn't know you liked birds so much," Ab said as he eased the saddle onto the back of his little black.

"Ummm," Johnnie said, "just wait till you see *this* bird. I'll show her to you, but *I* get her first."

"What do you mean 'first'?" Josh said as he pulled his latigo. "Is this gal a virgin—workin' at the Cattleman?"

Johnnie laughed. "When I've been out with the wagon this long, they're *all* virgins to me—soiled doves or not. . . . Will you hurry up, Josh?"

Josh turned his sorrel around, got on and said as he trotted past us, "I thought you wanted to rattle your hocks." All of a sudden, with those words barely out of Josh's mouth, his little sorrel swallered his head, squealed and went to pitching.

If the sorrel had pitched to match his squealing, he would have gone clear to the moon, but really all he was doing was jumping forward and landing hard on all four feet and kicking at Josh's spurs. Josh was yelling, "Whoa, you son of a bitch!"

When I saw Josh lose his right stirrup, I spurred my gray in front of the sorrel. Just as I got in front of them, Johnnie rode up to the left side and bumped his horse into the sorrel. This made the sorrel pull his head up and stop pitching and stand between us trembling and wide-eyed.

"What 'n the hell did you do that for?" Josh said as he got his right foot back into the stirrup.

"'Cause it looked like you were about to get farted off!" I said.

"This little sorrel bastard wasn't raised on the right kind of milk to fart me off!" Josh said in a huff.

"Well," Johnnie said, "I don't think the little sorrel here knows that. . . . I think he knew you blew that right stirrup just like me an' Casey did and—"

"Well, so what! What if I'd a blowed both stirrups, and what if I'd got my head stuck in the dirt! Do y'all think I'm too goddamn old to get back in the middle of this little bastard and spur the hair off 'im?"

"No," I said, "it just looked to me like you could use a hand. . . . But from now on whenever you get in a jam I'm just gonna ride off and let you go to hell. When I get in a bind though, I'd appreciate the hell out of a little help—I sure wouldn't bellyache about it!"

Josh pulled his hat down and reined the sorrel away from us. "Well . . . hell," he said as he rode out the gate.

It was snowing a little again, and as we were riding past the bunkhouse, Johnnie pulled up and said, "You don't reckon Billy's got another bottle of that Yellow Rose, do you?"

So we yelled to Billy, and he stepped out of the bunkhouse. "It's sure cold, Billy," Johnnie said. And Ab said, "And it's a pretty good trot to Tascosa—probably be colder by the time we get there."

We were all smiling and Billy was smiling and he said, "So do you boys want to borrow some more coats? . . . Or would you rather have a bottle of whiskey?"

"Uh . . . let me think," Johnnie said. "Okay, I've thought about it, let's have the whiskey."

Billy went inside, and in less than a minute he came

back out with another bottle of Yellow Rose—this one three-fourths full—and handed it to Josh.

We tried to pay him for it, but he waved and said, "You can just buy me a bottle in town tonight."

We rode east out of Alamocitas Camp along a barbed-wire fence that stretched before us as far as we could see. With the hundreds of miles of outside fence completed, fencing crews were busy building cross fences, slicing the range into pastures—some with no more than a hundred thousand acres in them.

"Watch that damn bobbed wire," Josh said in disgust. "It'll ruin a horse quicker 'n a bolt of lightning. Last year up at Buffalo Springs the remuda got to runnin' one night in a thunderstorm and ran over the outside fence. When we found 'em the next morning, five of 'em was cut up so bad we had to kill 'em."

We stopped and passed the bottle of Yellow Rose around—twice—and then we trotted on down the fence.

"It just goes to show you what can happen if a bunch of easterners gets ahold of a cow outfit," Johnnie said. "This is open-range country, always has been and always will be. Them old cowmen all know it, but I guess these foreigners will have to learn the hard way. . . . Fences just won't work in this country. Cattle have to be able to move around where nature calls 'em, where there's water and protection. . . . These goddamn fences just won't work."

"What if they do?" I said.

We pulled up and passed the bottle again.

"They won't—no way in hell will they work!" Josh said. "Cattle will tear 'em down gettin' to water."

"But that's why they're drillin' all these holes and

putting windmills over 'em," I said. "So the cattle won't have to travel miles and miles to a spring or to the river—at least that's the idea."

Josh handed me the bottle again and said, "Casey . . . you ought to drink more and talk less."

"They tell me that if lightnin' hits a fence it can travel down it and kill anything touchin' the wire—even miles away," Ab said.

"That's a hell of a crazy notion," Josh said. "But just supposin' it's true, it makes you wonder even stronger about why in the hell anyone would even think about buildin' a goddamn bobbed-wire fence on a cow outfit—they keep cattle from water; cattle die on 'em in blizzards, because they can't drift with a storm like nature intended; and now, if what Ab says is true, whenever there's lightnin' all the cattle standin' next to a fence drop over dead. . . . Now how smart of a goddamn feller does it take to figure out they ain't such an all-fired good idea."

We passed the bottle again, and Ab passed his Bull Durham around and we all rolled smokes and cussed fences and anyone who would build them and wondered how grown men could be so stupid. Finally Josh hit upon the most plausible explanation for such stupidity: "Inbreedin'," he said, obviously pleased with himself for being capable of such insight. "It happens in cities all the time, and no wonder too, when you've got that many people breedin' and multiplyin' and most of 'em just stayin' on the range they was born on instead of driftin' off like cowboys and critters do."

CHAPTER
3

One of the better-known remedies for the relief of the symptoms of end-of-fall-works melancholy is a careful mixture of cheap whiskey and good-natured banter. Although it can't be guaranteed to restore youth, vigor and vitality like the tonics and elixirs medicine-show peddlers hawk, it has been known at times to pick up an old cowboy who is a little down in the mouth. That same mixture had done that to me—picked me up . . . a little, that is. I still wasn't feeling exactly like I wanted to, or like I thought I ought to, but I wasn't wanting to go off by myself anymore and be alone either. I'd made myself stop thinking about home and the folks and all the things I'd seen and done, and I tried not to let myself think of the future either.

The past and the future are dangerous things for any cowboy to think about. You have to learn to be concerned only with the here and now and the hell with everything else. Most of us have no more past or future than an old stray dog anyway, so to dwell on either of them is foolish—and is also one surefire way of bringing on the melancholy. The trouble is, sometimes they creep in on a man unawares and silent, like soft cotton from a cottonwood tree that settles on a man's shoulders as he rides along a creek bank without him knowing it.

We rode along the fence for a couple of more miles before we came upon the fencing crew that was building it. We rode past them with only saying "howdy," not being inclined to stop and visit with men in the process of slicing up the range and who were thereby our inferiors. After all, we did *our* work from the back of a horse with leather and ropes, while they did theirs mostly on foot with pliers and diggers.

"Poor fellers," Josh said after we were almost out of earshot of the fencers, "their old mommas musta dropped 'em on their heads before they was weaned."

"Probably syphilitic," Ab said, "like old Crooked Gait Johnson. They say all fencers come out of insane asylums anyway."

Once we were past the end of the fence we bent toward the northeast, toward Torrey's Peak, a landmark that could be seen for miles and miles. The sun was still somewhere in the sky but hidden behind heavy clouds that had started spitting a little snow again.

When we were riding across some level country covered with tobosa grass called Torrey Flats, a couple of miles east of Torrey's Peak, we saw movement in the tall grass a mile east of us. When we got closer we saw an old shell of a cow fighting off two lobo wolves while another sat on a small rise and watched.

"She's as good as dead," I said. "She's already down in her ass end."

21

"That old she wolf on that knoll is as good as dead, too," Johnnie whispered as he slipped his rifle, an old .38–55 Winchester, out the boot underneath his right leg.

The grass was too tall for a man to lie on his stomach and shoot, so Johnnie stood in front of us, aiming offhand.

"That's two hundred yards, Johnnie," Josh said. "Don't you reckon you ought to save your bullets and just throw the rifle at her? You'd stand a better chance of hittin' her that way."

"Betcha five dollars to one," Johnnie said, squinting his left eye.

"You're on," Josh answered.

The Winchester exploded, bucked and belched a cloud of gunsmoke. The wolves froze for an instant with heads up, sniffing the air while Johnnie worked the Winchester's lever; then they lowered their heads and took off.

Johnnie fired again when the she wolf was halfway down the knoll. This time she jumped and yelped and started spinning in a tight circle, biting at her side.

When we got to her she was lying in the tall grass at the foot of the knoll, dead.

"Luckiest goddamn shot I ever saw," Josh moaned.

"Pay me," Johnnie said.

"We bet on the first shot, not the second," Josh grinned and said.

"Bull dip," Johnnie said. "Boys?"

"He's gotcha, Josh," I said.

Josh swung his leg over the cantle and stepped to the frozen ground, cut off the dead wolf's ears with his knife and handed them to Johnnie. "Here," he said.

"Whadaya mean 'here'?"

"I mean *here!* These ears are worth at least fiv
dollars, so we're even."

Johnnie held up the bloody ears. "But these were
already mine!"

"No," Josh said as he pulled himself back into his
saddle, "they belonged to that wolf until I cut 'em off.
That made 'em mine, and then I gave 'em to you,
which makes us even. . . . Boys?"

"I think he's gotcha, Johnnie," Ab said.

"This ain't right," Johnnie said.

"Okay, Johnnie, okay," Josh said, "it may not be
right . . . but it *is so*. We made a bet, I lost and I paid
you. Now quit your whinin'."

I rode over to the old cow. She was poor and weak
and hamstrung on both hindquarters. "She's wet," I
said, looking down at her bag and seeing her long,
chapped teats.

"Here's her calf," Ab said, looking down into the
tobosa grass nearby, "or at least what's left of it, which
ain't much but a little hide 'n' hair."

I stepped off the gray and held my Colt two feet
from the cow's head. She bellowed at me and slung
her head in fight, trying to reach me with her wrinkled
horns. There wasn't anything else to do. She wouldn't
last two days, even if the wolves didn't come back,
which they would. "Sorry, old momma," I said,
cocking the Colt, "it's the cold, the wolves or me—
hell of a choice, ain't it?"

"Come on, Casey," Josh said, "shoot the old thang
and let's go, my toes are colder 'n hell."

I pulled the trigger, and she stiffened, blew blood
bubbles out her nose, thrashed her legs and died. We

passed the bottle around again and trotted on, leaving the dead cow, what was left of her dead calf and the dead wolf lying silent in the cold on Torrey Flats.

Another drink of Yellow Rose and a mile later, on the east side of Torrey Flats nearing a steep rimrock, we spooked a bobcat out of a clump of bear grass. She had been eating a jackrabbit and didn't see or hear us until we were no more than ten feet away. She wasn't any more surprised than we were though, because we didn't see her until she shot up out of the bear grass. We boogered her and she boogered us. She hissed and went east, and our horses snorted and went west. It was all pretty Yellow-Rose-funny though, even before we got our horses' heads gathered up and slowed down. We'd drunk so much that we were easily entertained—nothing short of a disaster would have failed to have been humorous to us.

"We oughta rope that cat," I said.

"Betcha can't," Josh countered.

"How much?" I shot back, lifting the loop of the leather rope string off my saddle horn and grinning.

"A dollar."

"Five to one?" I said, shaking out a loop.

"Why not?" Josh said as he grinned and bit the end off a twist of Old Republic tobacco. "Havin' seen old gray there run and you rope I'd feel safe at a hundred to one, but you said five to one so we'll go with that."

I pulled my hat down, slipped the horn-loop end of my catch rope over the saddle horn and pulled it snug, gave the gray some rein and a touch of J. O. Bass spur steel, said to Josh, "You old fart," and took off.

By then the bobcat was high-lopin' through the grass with about a hundred yards of XIT real estate between us, which me and the gray had cut in half before she threw her stub of a tail in the air and decided she'd better see what the country below the rimrock was like as soon as was catly possible.

I knew my gray could run a hole in the wind—in spite of what Josh had said—but I *didn't* know the bobcat could, too. Most bobcats are quick, but not real fast—this one was both. The amount of country between us and the cat was getting smaller, but so was the amount of country between the cat and the rimrock.

I reached back and tapped the gray on the rump with my loop and then lifted it over my head and started swinging it. By then me and the gray were about three jumps from being close enough for me to rope, and the cat was about four jumps from the rimrock.

It wasn't quite the loop I had in mind, but when the cat got to the edge of the rimrock and the gray put on his brakes, I cranked my arm one more time and threw.

It was a sorry kind of loop, and I was glad Josh, Johnnie and Ab were behind me so they couldn't see just how sorry it was. But when it was almost out to the end of my rope and had closed up until it was about the size of my hat, it just happened to arrive at a certain midair point two feet past the edge of the rimrock at the same instant the bobcat did. It was like my loop and that bobcat had a midair appointment, like the cat had such a craving to get inside a hemp loop that nothing was going to keep her out of it even if she had to jump six feet to get to it.

Regardless of how it happened, the loop went

around the cat's neck at the last instant, and she flipped over backwards in midair, screaming and scratching and clawing.

"By God," I said, "there!" like it happened just like I'd planned it.

But when she came over backwards she also came *out* of the loop, either shucking it off with her scratching and clawing or just simply falling out of it. Regardless of how it happened, she came out of the loop just as quickly and with as much surprise to both of us as she had gotten into it.

The whole catch, flip and get-out couldn't have taken more than two seconds, and ten seconds after she'd escaped Josh, Johnnie and Ab came up beside me horseback, laughing like hell.

"I thought you an' old gray were gonna hell it right off this rimrock, Casey," Ab said, bending over his saddle horn in laughter.

"You should have," Johnnie said. "It ain't no more 'n a ten-foot drop."

I grinned and started coiling up my rope but didn't say anything.

"What'd you do," Josh said as he uncorked the bottle of Yellow Rose, "just throw your rope at her like it was a bucket of water?"

I finished coiling up my rope and dropped the coils over the saddle horn. Then I took a drink out of the bottle, wiped my mouth and cocked an eye toward Josh. "Well hell no, I didn't," I said. "I reached out and stuck it on her—right around the throat latch. You can wait till we get to town to pay me though—of course there'll be a little interest due if you do."

"Pay you hell!" Josh said. "You gotta catch her first."

"I did catch her! Didn't y'all see?"

"All I see," said Josh, "is your rope layin' there on your saddle . . . and damned if I can see a bobcat in it. Johnnie, can you or Ab see a bobcat in old Casey's rope?"

"Hell's bells," I said, "you all had to've seen it. . . . I roped her just as she jumped off the rimrock . . . roped her right around the neck, and jerked her straight over backwards."

"Then why in the hell is she runnin' down the middle of that dry creek bed way down yonder?"

"Because I didn't want you pullin' the same thing on me that you pulled on Johnnie. I figured that if I kept her in my rope you'd cut off her ears and say we were even. So at just the right time when she was comin' over backwards I gave her just enough slack so she'd fall out of my loop." I was proud of that spontaneous fabrication. If you couldn't stretch the truth, you'd better never bet with Josh.

"You've roped enough bobcats so you know exactly how to do that, huh?" Josh said with a certain amount of pride-wounding skepticism in his voice.

"Yeah," I said, "you're damn right I have. . . . I do it that way ever' time I rope a bobcat . . . *ever' time!*"

"Bullshit, Wills," Josh said, "you owe me a dollar."

"Bull catheron yourself," I said, speaking my own brand of Spanish, "you owe *me* five dollars!" Then I thought I'd better take my case to the jury—"Boys?" I said.

"We couldn't hardly see nothin' after you throwed, Casey," Ab said, "'cept old gray's ass."

"Well, thanks a hell of a lot, boys," I said.

"You can wait till we get to town to pay me," Josh

said with a cocky grin. "Of course if you do you'll owe a little interest."

"Why in the hell anybody would ever bet with you is beyond me," I said. "The only reason we bet with you in the first place is to give a little enjoyment to your miserable old life, and then you have to figure out some way to cheat us."

"And the only reason I ever bet with y'all is just to hear you whine. I lose to Johnnie and pay him off and he whines, and then I win a bet fair and square with you and you whine. My good nature tells me that I oughta just tell you we'll call our bet off and you don't owe me that dollar, but then that wouldn't help you to build any character. The next thing I'd know you'd be hangin' in some gallows somewhere and I'd blame myself for not developin' you proper and holdin' you responsible for fulfilling your obligations."

"Good God," Johnnie said as he stepped off his horse and started peeing off the rimrock. Then me and Josh and Ab got off and started peeing off the rimrock, too.

"You ain't got much pressure, Josh," Johnnie said.

"I got enough to empty my bladder and keep my boots dry while I'm doin' it," Josh said. "Anything more than that is a waste of human energy. I might could pee over the moon, but what more good would that do than peein' two inches past the end of my boots? . . . You oughta learn to be more like Ab, Johnnie. You see how he can just stand here and pee and mind his own business. And he's not always whinin' like you and Casey are either."

We all stepped back from the rim. Josh held out the bottle and looked at it and said, "Boys, we're in a hell of a jam. I figure we've still got six or seven miles of

country between us and town, and looky here . . .
we'll be lucky if we can get any more than three miles
out of this bottle."

"We'll die," Johnnie said. "I've heard of cowboys
fresh off the wagon who tried to trot that far without
any whiskey, but I've never heard of any of them ever
makin' it."

"Let's get goin'," Josh said as we moved to our
horses. "We may still have a chance if we hurry."

In a few seconds, we were three-fourths of the way
ready to strike a long trot but were waiting on the
other fourth. Josh was pulling himself into his saddle
like he was in a barrel of cold molasses. "Josh,"
Johnnie said, "will you promise us you won't get off
your horse again between here and town? . . . You
oughta learn to be more like Ab. Did you see how
quick and easy he got on his horse?"

During the next few miles the whiskey was rationed
so sparingly that we talked and laughed less and felt
the cold more. Shortly before dark we reached the
Canadian River at a point opposite and just above the
mouth of Cheyenne Creek and about three miles from
Tascosa. After riding across a quarter mile of smooth-
ly flowing red water shoulder deep to our horses, we
stopped on the north bank and witnessed the
inevitable—the plucking of the very last Yellow Rose
blossom from the bottle Billy Nye had given us.

Just after Josh tossed the empty bottle into the
waters of the Canadian with the requiem "And may it
rest in peace," Ab pointed downriver to the mouth of
Cheyenne Creek and said, "Looky yonder . . . there's
an old cow bogged down."

"Three million acres on this outfit," I lamented,

"and she has to wander right out into the mouth of a creek where she's a cinch to bog down. Sometimes I wonder if God ever created a dumber critter than a cow brute."

"I think He did," Johnnie said as we trotted toward the cow, "and He split 'em up the middle far enough so their legs would hang down on either side of a cow horse and told 'em to try to keep the cloven-hoofed beasts that graze upon the grass and wander into the bogs alive."

The creek wasn't running any water, but the sand in the mouth close to the channel of water in the river, where the cow was bogged down, was waterlogged, and the more you worked it up the more that water came to the surface.

Some cows want to live so bad they'll do everything they can to keep you from saving their miserable lives. That's the way the cow in the bog at the mouth of Cheyenne Creek was. She fought us every step of the way, ripping Ab's coat with a horn and making sure all of us—but Josh—got a nice uneven plastering of wet sand.

"That's okay, Josh," Johnnie said to him one time when he was down on his knees in the wet sand, "we'll get her out. Why don't you just sit up there and roll cigarettes?"

Josh grinned and said, "You're the one who said you didn't want me gettin' off my horse again before we got to Tascosa—remember?"

But we never considered not getting that cow out of the bog, even though it was getting dark and we were cold and on personal horses and wanting to get to town and had been off the company payroll since we followed the remuda into Alamocitas Camp several hours ago. All that mattered was that there was a cow in a bog and she would die if we didn't get her out. It wasn't loyalty to the outfit that made us do it, but loyalty to who and what we were—cowboys.

It took over an hour, but finally we were able to dig enough bog sand out from around the cow's rump to get a loop around it. With that loop and two more around her horns—and me down beside her poking her in the ribs with a short stick—we finally got her out. She was so grateful that before we could get all the ropes off her she hooked my gray in the butt hard enough to bring a little blood and make him go to pitchin', but the sand was so deep he couldn't do much but make a fool of himself. After we got lined out and headed to Tascosa again, I told Josh that probably even *he* could have ridden him—even without any help from me and Johnnie.

CHAPTER 4

There she is, boys," Ab said as we topped a knoll and saw the lights of Tascosa less than a mile away.

"Yeah," Josh said, "and don't she look lovely? You know, when a man's been sleepin' out under the stars and callin' a wanderin' chuck wagon home for a few months, makin' an honest livin' out in the wide open spaces where the air is clear and clean, he gets to thinkin' that he's got ever'thing in his life that he needs. But then he gets done and rides to town and tops a hill like this and sees the lights of a little cow town nestled along the banks of a river and he realizes there are some things that life on the range deprives a man of."

"I guess you mean barbershops and stores and . . . ," Ab said.

"Good Lord, son. . . . No, I don't mean barbershops and stores!" Josh said, chuckling. "Where'd you learn to punch cows? I'm talkin' about sin and wickedness, the two things God created towns for in the first place."

We rode on into town and checked our horses into the livery stable and ourselves into the Exchange Hotel, paying both proprietors in advance. Then, by unanimous vote, we decided to go next door for "a quick drink" before taking our baths.

"We'll be right back," we told the clerk. "Start heatin' the bathwater."

We stepped inside the Exchange Saloon and stopped amid a nice thick layer of smoke to look around. The place was crowded, not only with cowboys and saloon girls but with regular citizens, too, all of them laughing and talking at once and almost drowning out the piano player's rink-a-tink tune.

Two high-headed girls walked by and welcomed us with winks and big smiles.

"There's a couple of nice dries," Johnnie said.

"Ye-ah," I said, kind of drawing it out and looking at the girls from behind.

"Oh, they ain't perfect," Johnnie added, "but I figured they'd do for you and Ab."

"Now, boys," Josh reminded us, "no fighting. We don't want no trouble—that's not what we came to town for. Let's just step over to the bar and have a drink."

After we got our drinks, me and Ab and Johnnie stood there leaning on the bar not even talking to one another while Josh and the man on his right struck up a quiet conversation.

About the time we set our empty shot glasses back down on the bar, I heard Josh say to the man he was carrying on a quiet conversation with, "Where in the hell did you get a crazy notion like that? This is open-range country and that goddamn bobbed wire won't work here!" By that time we had probably been in the saloon a total of five minutes.

When we heard Josh say, "What in the hell would a goddamn Yankee fence builder know about runnin' a cow outfit in Texas?" I looked at Ab and Johnnie and said, "Is it just me or has their conversation already gone to hell?"

"Naw," Johnnie answered, "it ain't gone to hell yet, but I'd say it sure has deteriorated."

When the man standing at the bar on the other side of Josh said, "And what would a cantankerous, worn-out old fart like you know about anything!" Josh hit him and Johnnie smiled at me and said, *"Now* it's gone to hell."

It wasn't so much that we didn't appreciate the accommodations offered us by Oldham County for the next two days and nights as it was the fact that since we had already paid for two days' and nights' room rent at the Exchange Hotel it seemed like we should have been staying there instead of at the jail. We hadn't even had our baths or shaved or had more than one drink of whiskey!

After dark on our second night in jail, Johnnie walked to the only window in our cell, put his elbows on the sill, rested his head in his skinned-up hands and sighed. "All that beautiful sin and wickedness out there . . . and we're in here."

"Just think of all the money you're savin', Johnnie," Josh said as he lay on a bunk with his hands behind his swollen and bruised head.

When none of us responded to Josh's remark he said, "Bunch of whiny-babies . . . this ain't so bad—

not really. In a way, I'd think you boys would be sort of grateful: it's nice and warm in here, and we're gettin' fed twice a day, and we each got a bunk to sleep on—and it ain't costin' us nothin'. We've been in town nearly two days, and, thanks to me, we're not even broke yet."

"I guess if we're lucky enough, they'll keep us here till we die," Ab said. "Just think how grateful we'd be to you then, Josh."

"You'd die with money in your pockets," Josh told him. "Which is more than most cowboys can say. . . . Besides, I never asked you to help me."

"You're right, you never did," Johnnie said, still gazing at the window toward Main Street. "Of course, we were foolish enough to think that was only because that fencer had his fist in your mouth. We should have been able to tell that you were just fixin' to whip his ass . . . and his three friends' asses, too!"

"Damn right!" Josh said in an angered voice.

After a short spell of silence, somebody on the other side of the dark cell, either Johnnie or Ab, started laughing low. Before long all four of us were laughing loud, and we laughed until we cried and our sides ached.

"You four men have been charged with . . . let me see here"—the judge looked at some papers in front of him—"Here it is—you've been charged with disorderly conduct, fighting in a commercial drinking establishment and destruction of property. How do you plead?"

We looked at one another, and then I shrugged my shoulders and said, "Not guilty, Your Honor."

"That means there will have to be a hearing, and I

call that hearing to order right now and pronounce all of you guilty as charged. I fine you an amount equal to the estimated damages to the Exchange Saloon, which comes to a total of three hundred dollars, which is seventy-five dollars apiece, and sentence you to thirty days in jail—apiece. Since Billy Nye has told me you have jobs on the XIT, I'll waive the jail sentence if you can pay the fine and promise me you'll all be out of Tascosa in thirty minutes."

"But none of us have seventy-five dollars, Your Honor," I said.

"Uh-huh," the judge said, rubbing his chin. "How much do you have, sum total?"

We each pulled out our money and began counting it.

"I'd think you'd be grateful. . . . We got a bunk apiece and are fed twice a day, and it ain't costin' us nothin'—ain't that what you said, Josh?" Johnnie whispered.

"How much do you have?" the judge asked in an impatient voice.

"Two hundred and sixty-three dollars," I told him.

"Then that's what the fine is—two hundred and sixty-three dollars. Pay the clerk and get out of town, and remember—it's thirty minutes or thirty days. Case dismissed."

We saddled our horses in silence, our dispositions having been somewhat soured by the disheartening chain of events over the past couple of days.

"At least we still got jobs," Ab said as we rode west from the livery stable, down Main Street, into a cold west wind and toward the XIT. "And if we hit a long trot we should make it to Alamocitas just in time for supper."

As we were trotting past the Cattleman Saloon, Johnnie suddenly pulled up and said, "Gawdamighty, boys, I just thought of something . . . I ain't broke!" He reached into his coat pocket and pulled out the pair of wolf ears. "I still got these!"

"So what?" Josh said with a scowl. "Are you gonna go back to the courthouse—where that kindhearted old bastard of a judge is—and cash 'em in?"

Johnnie laughed. "No, Josh, I ain't. I'm gonna go in the Cattleman and trade 'em to Raven."

"Hell, Johnnie," I said, "let's go. What kind of a whore would take a pair of smelly old wolf ears? Besides that, the judge gave us thirty minutes to get out of town and that was at least twenty minutes ago."

Johnnie laughed as he stepped up onto the boardwalk. "Jealous-hearted bunch, ain't you?"

Ab had some Bull Durham left, and we each rolled two cigarettes and waited on our horses in front of the Cattleman in the cold.

"Hi, boys!" We looked up, and there was Johnnie leaning out a window above the Cattleman's veranda wearing absolutely nothing but a proud smile. "I'll be through here in a few minutes. Hope you boys don't mind waitin'."

"He must've made the trade," Ab said in a disappointed voice.

"Yeah," I admitted, "and we'll never hear the end of it either."

Josh laughed. "Yeah, we will too. Casey, give your reins to Ab, and come on inside with me."

There were about a dozen people inside the Cattleman, some at the bar and some sitting at tables.

"Which one of them rooms up there is that cowboy who just came struttin' in here in?" Josh asked the bartender.

"I think he went into room twelve, but—"

"Come on, Casey . . . here's what we're gonna do," Josh said as we headed for the stairs.

I'll have to admit, when I heard the plan I couldn't help but like it.

I stood next to the door of room number twelve and said in a loud whisper, "Johnnie . . . it's past time for us to leave and the sheriff is comin' up the stairs." Then I yelled, *"No, Josh . . . no!"*

Josh drew his old Colt revolver and shot straight up twice, putting two holes in the ceiling and emptying the bar.

We stood there in the hallway for a few seconds without moving or talking, trying to keep from laughing.

"Casey . . . Casey," Johnnie whispered from the other side of the door. "What in the hell happened?"

"Oh, my God, Johnnie!" I moaned. "Josh just killed the goddamn sheriff! Go out the window and we'll meet you at the horses. . . . Hurry!"

"Ho-ly shit!" Johnnie said, as Josh and I ran down the stairs.

We walked back across the bar floor and tipped our hats to the bartender.

When we were outside, we saw Ab reach out and catch a pair of boots and a bundle of clothes. Then we saw Johnnie swing down from the veranda and we heard our horses snort.

"I'd forgot how ugly a naked man could be," Josh said.

"So damn skinny and bowlegged," I said.

It was while we were helling it out of town and rode past Sheriff East—who was leaning on the rump of a black horse harnessed to a buggy, talking to a man and woman sitting on the buggy seat and unmistakably unfull of bullet holes—that Johnnie realized the ruse. Of course, when he looked back at the three of us eating his dust and grinning, he didn't look amused. For by then he was not only aware of the ruse but was also suddenly aware of the fact that people were stopping, looking and pointing at him as he rode full throttle down Main Street wearing nothing but a hat and a fresh suit of goose bumps.

When Johnnie reached Tascosa Creek just past the west edge of town, he turned down it and stopped between two small plum thickets to put his clothes on.

He didn't say a word while he dressed, and me and Ab and Josh had to get off our horses because we were laughing too hard to sit in our saddles. I leaned on my gray for support, and Josh got down on his knees. Ab finally had to just lie down in the sand of the dry creek bed.

"Goddamn, Johnnie," Josh said, when he was able to say anything at all, and it took him several tries to say this: "If it'll make you feel any better we'll ride back into town and kill that sheriff—or at least we'll try and kill *somebody* for you."

CHAPTER

5

Ab, Josh and Johnnie rode back to Alamocitas just about like they figured they would when they left—broke. The only difference being instead of leaving their money at the saloons and parlors they left it with the clerk at the courthouse, which, in the greater scheme of things, all works out the same. Broke is broke. Josh wouldn't need to take one of his Dr. Chaise's Nerve and Brain Pills as he usually did when returning from a spree in town though, so he could save a little there. The pills were guaranteed to cure, among other things which none of us could pronounce, "Diseases from Sexual Excess." We didn't know what that meant, but Josh swore by pills and had kept a bottle in his war bag for years—as far as I could tell, the same bottle.

By the time we got back, Johnnie had started speaking to us a little, that is until we would burst out laughing, which we would every time any one of us thought about him riding out of town naked. Very few plans work as well as that one had, and Josh considered himself a genius for having devised it.

I had planned on coming back with money left, but I came back just as broke as Ab, Josh and Johnnie.

"Guess we'll have to work awhile before we can pay you back for that whiskey," I told Billy in the bunkhouse after supper. "Thanks for tellin' that judge that we had jobs—it probably saved us from sitting out a stretch in jail."

"The thing is, boys," Billy said, "I stretched the truth a little bit with the judge—I'm afraid I can't keep but two of you on. With these fences goin' up, they say it shouldn't take as many cowboys, and they're tryin' to cut down on overhead every way they can."

"The place I'd start doin' that," Josh growled, "is with them goddamn fencers. . . . Are they lettin' any of them go?"

"Hell, I don't know, boys," Billy said, "but I doubt it. I'm sorry, but I can't work any more cowboys than they'll let me."

"Who you keeping on?" Johnnie asked.

"It don't matter to me—you're all good hands and I'd just as soon have one as the other. I guess you'll have to decide between you who goes and who stays."

"It's going to be hard to find work this time of year, Billy," Josh said.

Billy stood up. "You boys decide tonight and then let me know in the morning."

Josh shuffled the deck of cards lying on the table. "High cards stay . . . low cards ride. I'll cut first."

Josh cut a jack of clubs. Ab cut a six of hearts. Johnnie cut a nine of hearts.

"Looks like Ab's ridin' for sure and Josh is stayin' for sure," Johnnie said. "Casey, before you draw just remember that I've got an old, sick mother I've got to take care of."

"Yeah," I said as I reached for the cards, "so do I." I cut a queen of spades.

"Damn!" Johnnie said as he knocked the cards off the table.

"That's life," Josh said.

"Yeah, that's what I'd say, too," Johnnie said, "if I had a job. Now I don't have one—and thanks to you I'm broke, too."

"Aw hell, Johnnie," I said, "you'd have come back broke no matter what, and you know you would have."

"Let 'im whine," Josh said. "It's what he's best at."

"Why you old son of a bitch!" Johnnie said. You can call a friend that in a certain diplomatic manner and get by with it, but suddenly that wasn't the manner Johnnie was using.

"Well, goddamn," Josh said. Then he rose up and hit Johnnie in the mouth with his fist.

"Let's go outside," Johnnie said, wiping blood from his lip with the back of a hand while me and Ab looked at each other and rolled our eyes.

You have to do it. Two men want to fight, you got to let 'em—men of a certain breed, that is. There are no grievance committees on any cow outfit I was ever on, and sometimes fighting clears the air like a strong breeze clears the hanging dust from a powdery round-up ground and lets you see things in a different light. It depends on the men, and also whether they're fighting from frustration or for honor and principle.

They fought for a while with both getting in their

blows. Josh was heavier and more experienced, but Johnnie was twenty years younger and stronger.

They were both giving out, and Josh was giving out the fastest and the most, but I knew he'd never quit. Johnnie would knock him down, and Josh would drag himself back up. Josh's face was getting cut to ribbons and his ribs were taking a terrible pounding—but he didn't have any quit in him.

"Stay down, Josh," Johnnie said from a crouched position with heaving ribs and heavy-hanging arms.

"Nnnne-ver," Josh breathed as he pulled himself up again.

"Then, you old wore-out bastard"—Johnnie's words were still rough but now they didn't sound like they were being pounded out on an anvil, and they were coming through a mustache stretched wide in a smile—"let's ask Casey and Ab if we've fought long enough to just quit. Hittin' your old hard head is about like hittin' a bodark post and it's ruinin' my hands."

"O-kay," Josh said wearily, "let's . . . ask 'em."

"Well . . . I don't know," I said, yawning. "It was a pretty nice fight for a while, but then it sure started tailin' off—and it *is* cold out here. What do you think, Ab?"

"I think one of you oughta try shootin' the other 'n between the eyes, and see if that would pick it up any. . . . If that don't work, I think we oughta go to bed."

So we all started laughing again, and when we got inside the bunkhouse where it was warm, Johnnie said, "What were we fightin' about anyway?"

"You called me an old son of a bitch," Josh said, easing himself down on his bunk, "and I hit you."

"Oh yeah," Johnnie said. "But I've called you a son of a bitch before and you never hit me."

"Uh-huh—well, I'm keeping track, and from now on ever' tenth time you call me that, I'm gonna hit you."

Johnnie laughed, turned the damper down on the stove, blew out the lantern and said, "You crazy old fart. . . . Where are we going in the mornin', Ab?"

"Don't know," Ab said. "Wherever the wind blows us, I guess. . . . In what other line of work can you get this much romance and adventure?"

After a little while of lying in the dark, a match flared and Johnnie lit a cigarette and said, "Guess we could go into the bank-robbin' business."

"Guess so," Ab drawled. "I knew a couple of old boys one time who got into that line of work. They done real well at it for a while, too . . . till one day the decoratin' committee of some little old place took a likin' to 'em. . . . I think the committee was in charge of fixin' the town square up for a May Day celebration, and they'd been lookin' for something to hang in the old apple tree in front of the courthouse. Well, when that decoratin' committee seen them two old boys abackin' out of the bank after making a deposit of two hundred fifty grains of soft lead with the vice-president and withdrawin' somewhat more money than a hundred cowboys coulda had on account there that decoratin' committee didn't bother to look no further."

"I guess ever' line of work has its drawbacks," Johnnie admitted.

It got quiet inside the bunkhouse then, quiet enough so I could hear a coyote howling outside. In a few minutes Ab was snoring and Johnnie was breathing deep and steady like he was asleep, too.

I had my hands behind my head and was looking up toward the ceiling when Josh started playing his harmonica. He didn't play it very often, but when he did it was always pretty. That night he played "Shenandoah," and he played it real soft. He probably thought I was asleep like Johnnie and Ab were. But I wasn't asleep. The few words that I knew to the song would come into my mind whenever Josh's harmonica would come to a place it sounded like the words would fit in, and they made that bunkhouse seem like a pretty lonesome place all of a sudden: "Shenandoah —Shenandoah . . . How I long to see her . . . Roll away, you rollin' river . . . Oh, Shenandoah—Oh, Shenandoah, across the wide Missouri."

After Josh stopped playing and it had been quiet a little while again, I said, "Did you ever wonder what it would be like to have a home of your own somewhere, and have a wife and—"

"I had all that one time," Josh said.

"You did?" I said. In all the years I'd known him, that was the first time he'd ever said anything like that, and it sure surprised me.

"Yeah," he said.

"When and where was that, Josh?"

"It was a long time ago," he said, "and in a place a long ways from here."

"What happened?"

Josh didn't answer, and after another short spell of listening to Ab snore and that coyote howl outside, I said, "Do you miss her? Your wife, I mean."

"Casey. . . . Naw, I haven't even thought about her

in years. . . . Now we better go to sleep, Billy'll be puttin' us to work in the mornin'."

"What was her name? . . . Josh?" But Josh was asleep, or at least acting like he was.

I lay awake for quite a while, trying to picture Josh married and wondering why he'd never told me about it. When I finally did drift off to sleep, I did so with Josh's harmonica still playing softly and mournfully in my ear, the music coming, I knew, not from the bunk across the room but from a time long ago and from a place a long ways from the bunkhouse at Alamocitas Camp.

CHAPTER
6

The next morning after breakfast, Johnnie and Ab rolled their beds and left just as the cold sun started peeking over the eastern rim of the world. No long and sad parting, just a handshake and a "prob'ly see you somewhere, sometime" and they were gone. Cowboys come and they go; they do both so often no one lingers over reunions or farewells. To do otherwise would not only be tiresome but would also be a breach of cowpuncher conduct.

Josh and I went out to the saddle house to make some repairs to our gear that we hadn't had time to do during the long fall works. The repairs were needed for sure, but even if they hadn't been, we would have been at the saddle house waiting on Billy Nye, because you never hang around the bunkhouse on a cow outfit even if you don't have anything to do—it's embarrassing to be caught hanging around the bunkhouse doin' nothing after the wagon has pulled in, whereas hanging around the saddle house doin' the same kind of nothing is more respectable.

When Billy came out to the saddle house, he said to us, "Boys—what 'n the hell happened to your face, Josh?—I guess y'all will be winterin' at Trujillo Camp. Get your strings of horses out of the remuda and some eatin's from the commissary." He tossed a bottle of Old Crow whiskey to Josh and a box with several sacks of Bull Durham tobacco in it to me. "I know you're both broke—you can pay me back the first of the month.

"You know where Trujillo Camp is, don't you, Josh? Well, I want you and Casey to ride that goddamn fence ever' day north to the river and south to the caprock. The nesters across the line love to cut the wire and drive cattle into New Mexico. There's hammers and steeples and wire pliers in the barn. There's some windmill grease in there, too. . . . The windmills over there need to be greased ever' week or so—you may not know how to do it, but it ain't hard to figure out, just smear grease up there on the workin' parts where it looks like there was grease before. There should be some axes in the barn for choppin' ice when that needs doin', and there's some paint in the barn, too—for paintin' the outside of the barn and house.

"Whenever you find dead cattle, cut the ears off and save 'em—helps with the goddamn inventory, you know. And if you find something dead that ain't too rotten yet, skin it out and stack the hides behind the barn at the camp—a freight wagon will come by before spring and pick 'em all up and haul 'em to Tascosa, where they can be sold to a hide buyer out of Kansas. . . . When you run out of anything to do you can ride across the line into New Mexico and prowl around for stock that's wearin' this outfit's brand.

"The town of Endee is about twelve miles or so from Trujillo Camp—go south down the fence and just before you get to the caprock you'll see it a mile or two to the west, over in New Mexico—it's got a store and post office and hotel and cafe and bar and I don't know what all. . . . I've got things to do here, and there's a freight-wagon load of bobbed wire mired down somewhere in West Alamosa Creek that I've got to get some men and go help get out, so . . . I don't know when I'll be seein' you again. . . . That goddamn Findlay's still around here, so don't let him see you leavin' with that bottle of whiskey. . . . See ya later, boys."

"Whew." Josh was leaning on his saddle that was on a rack on the south wall of the saddle house. "I'm wore plumb out from just listenin' to old Billy tell about what all needs doin' at Trujillo. . . . I musta misunderstood him—he doesn't expect *us* to grease windmills and fix fence does he, Casey?"

"Mmmm—Sounds like it, don't it?" I said. "I guess it could be worse—we could have ridden out of here with Johnnie and Ab. At least we can get some food out of the company commissary and we'll have a roof to roll our beds out under."

"Well, it's a hell of choice, ain't it?" Josh said as he carried his saddle on his hip out the door of the saddle house and dropped it in the dirt of the corral. "If Billy hadn't of given us this whiskey, I think I'd a told him to take his goddamn windmills and his fence and go right straight to hell with 'em cause I was rollin' my bed and going to a *real* cow outfit."

* * *

We left Alamocitas Camp less than an hour later driving twenty head of saddle horses—our own personal horses in with them—and leading two more that were packing our beds and the food we got out of the commissary. The morning was chilly but it was sunny and still, and by the time we got to Loss Ess Creek the frost had disappeared off the sage and the grass.

It was about thirty miles from Alamocitas to Trujillo Camp, and we kept the horses in a long trot until we came to Mohair Creek, which was about two-thirds of the way. There we let the horses water and graze while we boiled some coffee, ate cold tomatoes from a can and then lay back to smoke.

A couple of hours later, I saw Trujillo Camp for the first time. I saw the windmill first, and then I saw the house and the barn, all of them rising up out of a broad flat where no trees or bush of any kind grew. There was a barbed-wire trap for the horses and a couple of corrals next to the barn. The barn and house were made out of thin, wide boards nailed onto upright two-by-four studs with strips of narrow one-bys nailed over the cracks where the wide boards came together. The barn had no floor, and the floor of the house was made of boards nailed into the foundation, which was heavy, horizontal timbers partially buried in the sandy soil. The roofs were tin, and the ceiling of the house, like that of the barn, went to the roof. The only door in the house was on the south side, and there was no porch, you just stepped up and out of the dirt into the house. The boards were unpainted and were weathering and graying on the outside but were still fresh on the inside.

A hundred yards west of the camp was the Texas–New Mexico boundary, which was also the west fence of the XIT—a barbed-wire fence that stretched as far as the eye could see both north and south. To the south you could see all the way to the caprock, the northern edge of the Staked Plains, a dozen plus miles away. You could see hills and small mesas between the camp and the caprock, but it was the caprock that loomed over them all. To the north you could only see a couple of miles, to the top of a sand-and-sage rise. To the west, across the fence, were more hills and more sand and sage, but not much else. Trujillo Creek was there, but it wasn't much of a creek until it crossed over into Texas three or four miles to the north. To the east, across the flat we'd driven the horses over, were low hills and salt grass and XIT cows and jackrabbits and antelope and those things that fed on XIT cows, jackrabbits and antelope.

"Here she is, Casey," Josh said as we stepped into the house carrying our bedrolls and two sacks of food. "Home, sweet home."

The house had two little rooms, and each little room had a single little window in the south wall. The room on the west had a stove, a sagging table, a lantern, two cowhide-bottomed chairs and an inch of sand in it; the room on the east had nothing in it, discounting the snake skeleton and empty whiskey bottle in one corner and the pile of cow chips and dried cactus pods in another corner, where a big pack rat had set up housekeeping.

"Not bad," I said.

We stayed busy just doing part of the things Billy had lined out for us to do. Trujillo Camp was about halfway between the Canadian to the north and the caprock to the south, and each morning when it was just barely light enough to see, one of us would saddle the night horse we'd kept overnight in the pens and jingle the rest of the horses in the horse trap. Then we'd catch a horse and split up to ride the fence, one going north and the other south, and we would swap directions each morning. Billy was right about the fence, it gave us a lot of hell—Josh said nearly every day that that was all fences were good for, anyway.

We would find a place now and then where it looked like the wires had been cut, but most of the time we spent repairing the fence, the damage was caused by livestock rubbing on a post and pushing it over or maybe a couple of bulls would get in a fight near it and before they had decided which one was the toughest they had laid down or tangled up a couple of hundred yards of barbed wire and broken off several posts.

After we would get either to the caprock or to the river, we would usually swing out to the east away from the fence and ride through cattle and check windmills and other waterings on the way back to Trujillo, which we would usually get back to about midafternoon. When we would get back to the camp, we would eat something out of a can, smoke a couple of cigarettes and drink a pot of coffee before catching another horse and leaving again. In the afternoons we would usually go together, maybe we would skin out a dead cow or drive a bunch of cattle away from a water hole that had dried up to one that hadn't.

Sometimes in the afternoon, we would find time to grease a windmill—which we always did together, with Josh holding the horses, cussing and declaring how we ought to quit and complaining how nasty of a job it was, while I climbed the tower with the bucket of grease.

When we'd get in at night, we would eat something out of a can, smoke a couple of cigarettes, drink a pot of coffee, have a shot apiece of Old Crow and crawl into our bedrolls.

The weather was staying pretty decent for that time of year—December—with bitter cold mornings but only chilly afternoons. It had snowed a couple of times, but they were light dustings only.

When I left home at sixteen, I was planning on going back soon, so I never bothered to write. Before I realized it, several years had slipped by and I'd drifted and done a few things I wasn't too proud of, and I guess I thought—if I thought at all—that it was too late to go home, or even write, so I never did either. But one night, after me and Josh had been at Trujillo Camp a couple of weeks, and with Christmas approaching and Josh playing his harmonica, I started thinking about home and the folks again. I started figuring up how long it had been since I had left and seen the folks or even heard from them—or them from me—and I couldn't believe it. I figured again, and again it came out the same. Where had all the years gone?

I lay in my bedroll a few more minutes listening to a cold wind rattle the loose panes in the windows of our shack and then got up, lit the lantern on the sagging table in the other room, dug out a broken stub of a pencil and a few sheets of writing paper out of my war bag.

"What 'n the hell are you doin'?" Josh asked.

"Writing a letter home," I answered.

"The hell . . . how long's it been?"

"A long time."

Dear folks,

I don't know if you are alive or dead, but if you are alive and get this letter, I know you will be surprised to hear from me. I am living at a place called Trujillo Camp on a ranch in the Texas panhandle with another cowboy named Josh Smith. I have never married, so you have no grandchildren from me. You could not understand the life I lead so I will not try to explain it now.

I think about you at times and wonder where all the other kids are now—scattered here and there, I guess.

This is all I know to write. It is not much after twenty-three years.

If you are alive and want to write a letter, I think I will get it if you address it to Casey Wills at Endee, New Mexico Territory.

Your son,

Casey

CHAPTER
7

The next morning was my time to ride south from the camp. After I had ridden all the way to the caprock on the little dun company horse that I called Dunny, I crossed the fence and rode toward Endee.

In all of my wanderings across the West I had seen a few towns as small as Endee, but I had never seen any smaller. Endee was the bare minimum size, I suppose, that it is possible for a town to be. How can any town be smaller than one having but a single structure? The post office, the hotel, the cafe, the store, the bar, all the things Billy Nye had mentioned were in one two-story frame building with a lean-to-type barn connected to the south wall.

The town—the building—had been erected beside a spring on the south side of a narrow draw. Two headstones were on the opposite side of the draw from the building. The caprock rose up to the south a mile or two and stretched as far as the eye could see toward the southeast and southwest; in every other direction there was . . . I guess there was nothing really, but a cowboy doesn't usually see miles and miles of wide open spaces as nothing. Endee was as much "in the middle of nowhere" as any town could be, but I had discovered, in my long years of drifting across the prairies and mountain ranges of the West, that "nowhere" had at least a hundred lonesome middles.

A big cottonwood tree with a few brown leaves still hanging on to the tips of its branches was in front of the building, the front being east. Underneath the cottonwood was a long hitching rail where two horses were tied.

I tied Dunny to the hitching rail alongside the other two horses, stepped up on the porch with a jingle of spurs and opened the door to Endee.

The bottom floor was one big room, with square timbers spaced throughout to support the second floor. To the right was the bar, with a man behind it cleaning glasses. Out from the bar were five tables, all with empty chairs at them but one, where two men were playing dominoes. Directly across the room was the staircase and the cooking stove. In the center of the room was another stove, this one a big, potbellied one for heating. To the left of the stove were three rows of tall shelves filled with canned goods and dry goods. The left wall, the south wall, had another long counter in front of it. A dark-haired woman sat at one end of the counter and behind it on a tall stool. She was writing in a big ledger and above her hung a sign which read: HOTEL REGISTRATION. Above the other end of the counter hung another sign:

U.S. POST OFFICE
ENDEE, NEW MEXICO TERRITORY

I stepped over to the counter where the woman was, and when she looked up from her ledger I tipped my hat to her. Her eyes were as dark as her hair. They were pretty eyes, and bright, but they had a certain sadness behind them, too.

"Hi, would you like a room?" she asked.

"No, ma'am," I said, reaching inside my coat and bringing out the letter I'd written the night before. "I'd like to mail this."

"Then you'll have to go to the post office," she said as she slid off her stool and moved to the other end of the counter.

I handed her the letter. "West Virginia, huh?"

"Yes, ma'am. It's to the folks. I don't know if they will write to me or not, but I told them that if they did they could send a letter here and I would probably get it. . . . My name's Casey Wills and I'm livin' at Trujillo Camp across the line on the XIT."

"Why wouldn't they write, Mr. Wills?"

"It's been a long time," I said. "I don't even know but what they might be dead—maybe for years."

The corners of her mouth turned up in a faint smile. "Well, Mr. Wills, my name is Lillie Johnson, and if you get any mail I will hold it for you."

"I'd be much obliged," I said.

"That'll be two cents . . . postage on your letter."

I smiled, embarrassed. "Sorry, ma'am, but right now I don't have it. I could wait till payday to mail it, but I kinda wanted it to get there by Christmas. . . . If you could give me credit I'll sure be good for it."

"It won't get to your folks until quite a while after Christmas, even if you mail it now—the stage just comes once a week."

"I see . . ."

"But I'll pay the postage on it myself, Mr. Wills. I'll take your word that you will come back and pay me."

"You can count on it," I promised.

A man leaned over the railing upstairs and said, "Lillie, have you got that ledger book straightened out yet?"

"Almost," she said. "I'll bring it up soon as I'm finished here."

"Looks like you and your husband have a pretty good business here," I said. "At least you seem to be doing better than any other place in town."

She smiled faintly again, and I tipped my hat to her and started to turn around and leave.

"Mr. Franks is not my husband," she said. "My husband's dead. He died back east, and I came out here to start my life over."

"Sorry, ma'am," I said. "I'll be back and pay you soon as I can. I appreciate the loan."

I stepped outside and was standing on the porch rolling a smoke when four riders came trotting up. They tied their horses to the hitching rail, and then one of them, two inches taller than me and built like a bulldog, with jaws as big as a studhorse's, walked all the way around my dun, looking at him. When he was finished looking, he said, "What'll you take for him?"

"He's not mine," I said. "He belongs to the company."

"XIT, huh?" he said, looking at the brand on the dun's right thigh. "You stayin' at Trujillo Camp?"

"Yeah."

"Well, I'll give you ten dollars for the little sorry bastard, and you can tell the company he died."

I licked my cigarette paper and didn't say anything.

"What's the matter?" Square Jaws said. "Is the XIT payin' its cowboys enough now so they don't need a little extra cash?"

"I've never seen a cowboy who didn't need a little extra cash," I said, "just like I never saw one who was worth a damn sell a company horse and lie about what happened to him."

"Hell—they'll never know but what the horse ain't dead."

I drug a match across my chaps, and when it flared I lit my cigarette. Then I said, "I'd know."

The man shrugged. "I don't like 'im, anyway. Probably ain't worth ten dollars." Then, with a deplorable lack of foresight, he goosed Dunny in the belly just behind the flank cinch with his thumb.

Dunny snorted, dropped an ear, jumped sideways and kicked, just like he should have. And he kicked not only with incredible swiftness but with acceptable accuracy to boot, planting a hoof neatly on Square Jaws's thigh with a satisfyingly loud whack and sending him sprawling in Endee's cold and dusty street.

I grinned as I unwrapped my bridle reins from the hitching rail. "How do you like 'im now?" I asked.

As I trotted away I heard the man call out—"Cowboy!"

I stop Dunny and turn him around and I'm looking into the embarrassing end of a Winchester. Behind the cocked hammer I see Square Jaws smiling. "You asked me how I like the dun now? Well . . ."

He squeezed the trigger. The rifle erupted with fire and gunsmoke. Dunny shook his head, and I felt light-headed, wondering how long it is before you feel pain once you've been shot.

While I was waiting for the inevitable—either an agonizing pain or the world going black around me—the man lowered the rifle, laughed and said, "I like the dun fine . . . *now.*"

Then I notice the .44 caliber hole in Dunny's left ear.

"Well . . . Good God!" I said that mostly on Dunny's behalf. For my part, I was much more relieved than depressed over that little hole. In fact, and under the circumstances, it was about the prettiest little hole I'd ever seen, and I was nothing but satisfied having it there.

I quickly weighed my options, and as I saw it I had two of them: I could make a big deal out of that one little hole in Dunny's ear and, considering that I was outnumbered, get myself shot full of holes and go down in Endee's legend, not to mention its graveyard. The only other thing I could do was to be discreet and charitable. It didn't take long to come to a decision, and it's amazing how easy it was to be discreet and charitable when you're outnumbered.

"Well . . . ," I said, "I'd like to stay and chat, but I've got some cows to take care of over in Texas. If you're ever in my neck of the woods, stop by and we'll have a drink. I'll even gather the horses and we can stand around and shoot holes in their ears."

"How'd it go this mornin'?" Josh asked when we met back at Trujillo Camp.

"Oh, fine," I said as I stuffed wood into the stove. "I rode over to Endee to mail that letter and had to borrow two damn cents from a woman for postage."

"Anything else?"

"Yeah," I said, "before I left town on old Dunny

some son of a bitch shot a hole in his left ear with a rifle."

Josh wrinkled his brow. "Why in the hell did he do that?"

"Thought it helped his looks, I guess—at least, that's what he said."

Josh looked somewhat confused. "That's a crazy goddamn notion. Did you see him do it?"

"Well, hell yes, I seen 'im do it. . . . I was sittin' right in the middle of him, by God!"

"Wait a damn minute, Casey. . . . This crazy man shot himself in the left ear while you were sittin' in the middle of him because he thought it would help his looks?"

I laughed. "No! He shot *Dunny* in the left ear while I was sittin' in the middle of him—of *Dunny*, dammit!"

"This man shot *Dunny* in the left ear while you were sittin' on him?"

"Yeah," I said. "That's what I've been sayin'."

"Well . . . goddamn," Josh said, and the rest of the day he was nearly blind—from laughing.

That night as we lay in our bedrolls in the dark, Josh said, "Did they have any women at Endee?"

"Not the kind you're talking about," I said.

"What kind did they have?"

"I just saw one—the one who works there and loaned me the two cents. She's got dark hair and dark eyes with high cheekbones and a pretty mouth."

"Carryin' a lot of flesh?"

"No."

"Gant?"

"No—just about right."

"She married?"

"She's a widow. Husband died back east."

"Did you tell her all the indecent things you'd like to do to her?"

"She's a lady, Josh."

"So you just thought it, huh?"

I laughed. "Yeah . . . I just thought it."

A few minutes later I said, "What happens to men like us, Josh?"

"What do you mean?"

"You know what I mean. What are you going to do in a few years?"

"You mean when I get so old and stove up no outfit will hire me?"

"Yeah. . . . What happens to men like us then?"

"Well, if we ain't lucky we wind up slingin' hash or sweepin' out saloons for whiskey and keep."

"And what happens if we *are* lucky?"

"In that case, Casey . . . some horse falls on us and breaks our goddamn neck before we get plumb wore out."

"Nice set of options, ain't it?"

"Yeah. . . . Now let's go to sleep."

"You said you were married one time . . ."

"That was a long time ago, Casey."

"Yeah, I know. . . . In a place a long ways from here. Was her name Anna?"

"How'd you know that?"

"I've heard you say that name in your sleep a couple of times."

"You have?"

"Yeah. . . . Why don't you go back . . . ?"

"There ain't no going back to them kinds of things, Casey. They ain't like a country you've been to one time and you can just go back to any time you want and ever'thing, creeks and canyons and draws, will be the same as they were when you left. You try goin' back to *that* kind of country and you find the creeks are too high and the canyons too deep to cross anymore. Now go to sleep, dammit."

I hadn't been asleep but a few minutes, I don't think, when I was woke up by the night horse we had in the pens nickering. Then I heard someone just outside yell, "Hello, in there!"

"That's that square-jawed son of a bitch that shot the hole in Dunny's ear," I whispered to Josh as we slipped into our clothes.

"I'll stay by the window, just in case," Josh whispered. "Better watch yourself."

I opened the door and stood in it holding my rifle. There was a half moon in the sky, which made it light enough to see decent. Square Jaws and his three compadres were sitting on their horses in front of the house.

"Didn't mean to disturb your sleep," Square Jaws said. "We kinda got off to a bad start today at Endee. My name's Tatum Stagg. This here's Eddie, Matt and Nate. Can we get off and come in and palaver?"

"I reckon we can do whatever palaverin' needs done right here," I said.

"We wanted to talk business," Stagg said.

"Like you did this mornin' at Endee? How is the ear-shootin' business anyway?"

"Look, I'm sorry about that. It's just that I hate everything about the XIT and what they stand for so much. And that stupid dun horse . . ."

"Did just what he should have done to somebody who didn't have any better sense than to goose him in the belly."

63

"Let's forget it—and you don't need to be afraid to go back to Endee."

"I was worryin' like hell about it," I said.

"Look, let's just forget it."

"It's forgot."

"I came here mostly on business . . ."

"You conduct your kind of business in the moonlight, do you, Stagg?"

"You said you'd never seen a cowboy who couldn't use a little extra cash."

"That ain't all I said."

"This hasn't got anything to do with horses."

"You got a way of hem-hawing around, don't you?"

"All right. . . . I'll pay you to just look the other way at times—you and that feller behind the window there too. Sometimes you might see a place where it looks like some cattle have been drove over the fence into New Mexico. The fence won't even be down, just maybe a few tracks. You pay no mind to it and I'll pay you—in cash—twenty dollars a week apiece."

"Mister," I said, "you came to the wrong camp."

"Don't be a fool. How many cows does the XIT have? A hundred and twenty thousand?"

"Give or take five or ten thousand," I said.

"Who's gonna know if a few of 'em get through this goddamn fence and disappear?"

"Me and Josh, for two."

"What's the XIT ever done for you? They'll work you to death and spit on your grave."

"You've had your say, Mister, and I've had mine. I saw in Endee that we like a different kind of horse, and I don't see any different now."

"You know, I never asked your name."

"Casey Wills."

"Casey, look . . . I know you're broke. I know you had to borrow two cents for postage. I've got money in my pocket, and I own my own place a few miles west of Endee. You keep workin' for cowboy wages and you'll never have either of those things. Do you think I got what I've got by giving my body away to some outfit that would use me up and then cull me like they would an old cow?"

"No . . . I think you got what you've got by givin' away something other than your body."

"I don't understand your kind of man, Wills."

"Yeah . . . well, I understand your kind. . . . I'm sorry you can't stay longer, but I know you and your men want to get back underneath your rock before mornin'."

"If you change your mind, look me up. I'm not bein' underhanded about it—I'm telling you straight out that I'm gonna steal from the XIT just like a lot of other people are doing. Even if we're caught, no jury out here will ever convict us. We're not stealin' from cattlemen like Goodnight or Chisum or Reynolds. We're stealin' from foreigners and corporations, investors and capitalists from back east or even overseas who want to crowd out the little man and own the whole goddamn world. To them a cowboy is just a piece of equipment like a pair of fencin' pliers or a windmill tower. Do you think they'll take care of you like you take care of them? I'm givin' you a chance to have something, which is more than you'll ever get from them.

"I'm not askin' you to steal—all you've got to do is grease windmills, fix fence and whatever else that fat board of directors in Chicago tells you to do. And you can take care of their cows too, just like you always have—as long as they're on the Texas side of the fence; we'll take care of the ones that wind up in New Mexico for you and pay you three times what they do. You can live on the wages they pay you and stuff what you get from me in a lard can. . . . Think about it, Casey."

"Your rock's gettin' cold."

"What's the matter, is what I'm saying startin' to make sense to you?"

"Rattle your goddamn hocks, Stagg," I said, levering a shell into the Winchester's chamber.

"Someday," Stagg said as he began reining his horse around, "when you're old and wore out and wonderin' how you're gonna eat for the rest of your life, you'll think back with regret to the time when you could've had something but passed it up. Opportunity doesn't knock on a cowboy's door every day, Casey. . . . And you wouldn't be the first XIT hand I gave a start to, either. I could take you to see a couple of hands who used to work for your outfit right now, you might even know them. They're not following some chuck wagon around anymore, and they're not livin' at some lonesome line camp hoping they don't get laid off before they can save up enough money to get drunk on. They're sittin' on their *own* little places, and they have 'em stocked with a nice little herd of their own cows. You don't think that board of directors in Chicago helped 'em get those places, do you? . . . Of course you don't. You *know* better than that, don't you, Casey?

"I'll tell you what. . . . Now don't get nervous with that rifle, I'm just getting something out of my pocket." He dropped something on the ground in front of his horse. "That's yours," he said, "yours and your partner's. You don't owe me nothin' for it. Let's just say it's my way of makin' up for shooting a hole in your horse's ear this mornin'."

As the riders were riding away and slowly blending into the moonlit landscape, Josh came up beside me and together we watched them disappear.

"What 'n the hell kind of callin' card do you reckon he left?" Josh said as he stepped out of the house to get it.

"Looks like money, Casey," he said as he looked at it in his hand in the moonlight. "Rolled up and tied with a string. Light the lantern."

Josh was right—it was money, a hundred dollars in cash.

"I'll . . . I'll put it in this empty Arbuckles can for now," Josh said. "The next time we see the bastard we can give it back to 'im."

"Yeah," I said, looking at the roll of money. "Put it there—till we can give it back to him."

CHAPTER
8

The next morning Josh and I had little to say as we sat at the table waiting for daylight, drinking coffee and rolling cigarettes. On the table between us was the Arbuckles can, silently holding the one hundred dollars in greenbacks that Stagg had dropped on the ground the night before.

"That money's like a pretty woman, ain't it, Casey," Josh said, his eyes riveted on the can. "One that's showin' more hide than clothes and smilin' at you in that certain way a woman can that says she's willing. . . ." Josh held a match to his cigarette, and for an instant our eyes met and then we both looked at the can again. Then he went on, "But you know she belongs to another man and oughtn't to be there at all, just like you know you ought not to touch her. . . . Still, dammit, no matter what else you try to think of and no matter where else you try to look, she's all you can see, and all you can think of is how it would feel to run your fingers over her skin and . . ."

I stood up and threw a rag over the can. Josh and I looked at each other, and in a second or two we both grinned.

"Looks like it's startin' to get light outside," I said. "Ain't it your turn to jingle horses?"

I got back to the camp that afternoon before Josh and was stuffing wood in the stove when he stepped inside the house.

Josh took off his gloves and his coat and threw them in the corner. Then he reached into his pants pocket and pulled out a twenty-dollar bill. He held it up for me to see and said, "Found it tied to the top of a fence post."

"I'll be damned," I said in amazement. "Was the fence out?"

"No . . . and it hadn't been cut—there was just one set of horse tracks on the other side of the fence and"—Josh held up the money again—"this."

"Stagg, huh?" I said.

"Do you know anybody else who would donate money to the Cowboys' Pension Fund? Maybe it's the XIT?"

I grinned at how ridiculous that possibility was and then said, "We'd better go see him and get this stopped."

"Had we, Casey? Are we doin' anything wrong?"

I shrugged. "We haven't done anything wrong yet, but you know what Stagg's got in mind."

"Just because he's got it in mind, don't mean we'll let it happen, but look here, Casey"—Josh stepped to the table and poured out the Arbuckles can and tossed the other twenty on top of it—"there's a hundred and twenty dollars here—"

"Bribe money," I said.

"Cash money," Josh said. "It ain't bribe money 'less we do something wrong—which we ain't done."

"Josh. . . . We can't keep it and you know we can't. Remember what you said this morning about the money being like a pretty woman in skimpy clothes . . . but a woman who was spoken for by someone else. Adding the twenty is like she just took off some *more* clothes—it don't all of a sudden make it right."

Josh grinned. "Naw. . . . You're right, Casey. . . . But I'll tell you one thing—we'd better get her dressed and send her home damn quick before she peels off somethin' else. Even the most Christianized man in the world has a limit on the amount of bare skin his system can tolerate before he starts pawin' the ground and bellerin'."

The next day was my time to ride the fence toward the south. "I'll ride over to Endee tomorrow," I said. "Maybe Stagg will be there."

The coffee was boiling on the stove by then, and I poured us each a cup.

"Makes a man wonder though, don't it, Casey?" Josh said.

I knew what he meant—just how much more money Stagg would throw at us. "Yeah," I said, "it makes a man wonder, all right."

The next morning when I stepped out of the house to jingle the horses it was cloudy and colder than hell, with a breeze blowing out of the north that was about as gentle as a wolf fang tearing at the flesh of a calf's flank. "Damn," I muttered as I turned my coat collar up and walked on out to the barn.

The horses were on the back side of the trap, and by the time I drove them into the pens my ears ached, and when I stepped off the jingling horse my feet felt like they would crack.

Josh stepped out of the saddle house and handed me the bottle of Old Crow that Billy Nye had given us the morning we left Alamocitas. "Better have a warmer-up." We had been frugal with the Crow ever since we'd been at Trujillo, limiting ourselves by nothing more than an awesome display of willpower to no more than a small swallow or two a day, but still the Crow had about all "gone south."

I took a small drink while Josh drug his saddle out of the saddle house and built a loop in his catch rope. "Catch me old Anvil Head," I said as I recorked the bottle. "My damn fingers are so stiff I don't think I can even hold a loop."

Josh threw a terrible loop at the horse and missed, mostly because of the rheumatism in his right shoulder. "Good God!" I said. His second loop was a pretty decent one that fit, but of course I didn't say anything about it.

While I was saddling Anvil Head, Josh caught a tall sorrel brainless wonder that he called Plato. Plato was a stupid and worthless hunk of XIT horseflesh even on a warm summer morning. I could imagine what he would be like on a cold winter morning. I hated to see Josh catch him, but it was Plato's turn to go, and I knew Josh would feel like he was giving in to age and rheumatism if he caught anything else.

When Josh swung his saddle up, Plato snorted and jumped sideways. The saddle landed on the ground, and Josh, being thrown off balance, fell on top of it.

This boogered Plato even more, and he jerked the reins through Josh's hand and ran back to the other horses.

As Josh was getting up we looked at each other. I could see how mad he was.

"Nice, ain't he?" I said.

"A real wonderful son of a bitch," Josh grumbled.

"Why don't you let him go to hell and catch something else?" I said.

Josh looked at me a few seconds and then said, "Goddammit, Casey." I knew what he meant. I knew what he felt. I didn't say anything else.

By the time Josh had caught Plato again, I had Anvil Head saddled.

Josh put his hobbles on Plato while I ran the rest of the horses into the next pen. While he was saddling up, I had time to trot old Anvil Head around and warm him up a little. You never can tell for sure what any horse will do, but I figured Plato was going to be pretty humpy when Josh finally got on him, and I wanted all the kinks out of my horse if he was. I didn't want to have to worry about both horses pitching. If a man has to help another feller out of a jam, it sure helps if he's not in one himself.

Josh took his hobbles off old Plato and turned him around. Plato was swelled up like a toad and tiptoeing like a ballerina.

"Why don't you tie your reins up and run the son of a bitch around the lot a few times?" I suggested. "Let him pitch with an empty saddle if he wants to pitch as bad as he acts like he does."

Josh gathered his reins up and looked at me hard. "Why? Because you don't think I can—"

"Dammit, Josh!" I said. "Why don't you knock it

off? I suggested it because that's probably what I'd do if that was my wood on old Plato. That's probably what *you* would do too, if you didn't think you had to keep proving something just because you're older than I am. . . . Well, you're damn right you're older than I am! You're *twenty years* older than I am, but there ain't no glory or extra pay for lettin' a hammerheaded son of a bitch like old Plato buck you off, no matter how old you are!"

That all made sense to me, but I could tell by the look on Josh's face that it was about the worst possible thing in the whole world that I could have said. He hitched up his britches, cheeked up old Plato and put his foot in his oxbow stirrup as deep as he could. "Just because you'd be afraid of this counterfeit bastard don't mean I am, Wills," he said. "You really don't think I can handle him, do you?"

I was aggravated by then. "No, by God, I don't! But I told you when me and Johnnie tried to help you at Alamocitas that the next time I was just gonna ride off and let you go to hell, and that's what I'm gonna do!"

"Well, just get your ass over there on the other side of the pen and stay outa the way then!" Josh said as he started up.

Josh was bundled up in clothes, but even if he hadn't of been, his reflexes and his coordination weren't what they had been at one time, weren't what they should have been to get on a cold-backed horse like old Plato on a morning when the temperature was in the teens. I knew that, and I should have planted my horse right in front of Plato. Instead, in aggravation, I had reined Anvil Head away and had my back to Josh when the wreck started.

Behind me I heard the inaugural sounds of nearly

every pitching that's ever taken place in a cow country—a hard passing of belly gas and the stretching and popping of saddle leather.

By the time I looked back Josh was already in trouble. Plato was pitching and spinning fast to the right while Josh was still trying to get on him. His left foot was still deep in the stirrup, while his right leg was on Plato's rump. He was trying to get on, but with Plato spinning away from him it was impossible to do. Josh was out there in no-man's-land, where you can't get on and you can't get off.

Josh wasn't saying anything, but I wheeled my horse around and hollered as loud as I could, "Whoa, you son of a bitch!"

I was going to ride in as close as I could and grab ahold of Plato, or at least try to ride into him and stop him from spinning—by then, spinning was about all he was doing, but he was spinning *fast!*

Before I could get to him though, Josh lost his grip on the saddle horn and was thrown away from the horse. . . . But his left foot didn't come out of the stirrup!

Josh was hung up!

No two words can run a chill down a cowboy's spine any quicker than *hung up* can. Of all the many hazards of the profession, by rope or by stirrup, being hung up is the most dreaded.

Plato's spinning suddenly became more intense. No longer was he simply cold-backed and mad at the fact that he was going to be ridden. Now he was snorting-kicking-spinning, wide-eyed scared. And where he might have held something in reserve in an effort to get the cowboy off his back, now he was using every single ounce of muscle and bone and brawn to protect himself from the demon dangling suddenly and strangely down at his side.

I spurred old Anvil headlong into Plato.

We hit Plato hard enough to knock him to his knees—but only for a second. Josh hadn't been hurt yet, not really, but his foot was still in the stirrup, and the instant he wiggled it in an effort to get it loose, Plato cocked an ear, kicked at him and took off again, this time not spinning but running and kicking.

I spurred Anvil Head up to Plato's right side, where I managed to grab the reins and dally them around my saddle horn. This stopped him from running—but not from squealing and thrashing and kicking. He twisted his butt around to the left, which put Josh underneath him, where he could *really* be stomped and kicked.

For an instant Josh tried to keep his arms over his head, but then I saw him go limber, his arms and head flopping like a rag doll's while Plato kept jerking him and kicking at him.

"Gawdamighty!" I said. *"Whoa, Plato, whoa!"* I was scared. Josh's foot wasn't going to slip out of the stirrup as one usually will after a second or two. And no amount of sweet talk, no amount of scolding, no amount of jerking was going to stop Plato from kicking and stomping. Even as hardheaded as Josh was, one solid lick by any one of those four stomping, kicking hoofs would cave in his skull.

Plato *had* to be calmed down—and *right now!*

I knew of only one way to save Josh. I put my .45 just underneath Plato's right ear and fired.

CHAPTER
9

As luck would have it, when Plato fell he didn't collapse on top of Josh but rolled over onto his right side, leaving Josh unmashed but lying facedown with his foot still in the oxbow.

I jumped off Anvil and, still scared and shaking, pulled Josh's foot out of the stirrup and gently rolled him over, dreading what I might see.

Josh's eyes were closed, and his face was skinned up even worse than it had been after Johnnie got through pounding on it outside the bunkhouse at Alamocitas some two weeks earlier. But I could see no caved-in places or any exposed skull or brains. None of his limbs appeared to be broken.

In a few seconds, Josh opened his eyes, and they seemed to focus on me. He let out a long sigh, like a man will do when he comes up from being underwater for a long time, and said, "Damn," softly and with a smile—a pained smile.

I let out my own long sigh as I sat down on Plato's

dead belly with my elbows on my knees, letting my brain and nerves settle. In a few seconds I looked over at Josh and said with a wide grin, "Nice damn wreck, Josh."

Josh dragged himself over to Plato's butt and leaned against it. While he began locating all the freshly acquired sore places on his head and body, I got the nearly empty bottle of Old Crow from where it was lying in the dirt by the saddle house door.

There was one drink apiece left, and when that was gone I sat the empty bottle upright on the flat of Plato's hip. "You okay?" I asked.

"Why, hell yes, I'm okay!" he said, like I was a fool for even asking. "Just a little sore is all."

"Maybe you ought to stay here today," I said. I expected him to argue, but instead he just nodded his head and said, "Yeah . . . I guess I ought to. . . . You'd have thought old Billy would've given us more than one bottle of whiskey, wouldn't you?" Then he started searching his pockets for his makin's. I pulled mine out and handed them to him.

"I'll help you get your saddle off old Plato here, and then when I get back we'll put a couple of horses in that harness in the barn and drag him off. . . . You sure you're okay?"

"I'm okay, dammit!" But when he stood up with a cigarette hanging out of his mouth, he didn't straighten up all the way, and he couldn't walk without limping or holding his back.

When I got back to Trujillo that afternoon, I expected to find Josh in the house, either lying on his bedroll or sitting at the table drinking coffee, but he was doing neither. In fact, he wasn't in the house at all. He wasn't even at the camp—and his saddle was gone, too. I figured he must have got to feeling better, decided to ride the fence and would be back before long. As I was sitting at the table waiting for the coffee to boil, I glanced out the window and noticed that it was snowing a little.

As I drank my first cup of coffee and smoked my first two cigarettes, the snowfall outside kept getting heavier and heavier. By the time I had finished my second cup, the ground outside was white and the wind was beginning to rattle a loose piece of tin on the roof. The house was getting colder, too, even though I had a good fire going in the stove.

I walked to the window and looked to the south. The caprock and the small hills and mesas had disappeared behind a fuzzy white veil. I kept my eyes on the fence at the spot where it disappeared in the snowfall, which was no more than a mile away, hoping to see Josh trotting in. "Come on, Josh," I said out loud. "Where in the hell are you?" Ordinarily, I wouldn't have been worried, but I knew he wasn't in much shape to ride, much less to be caught out in a snowstorm, which, by then, looked like what was settling down on us. "Why in the hell didn't you stay at the house like you said you were goin' to?"

In another fifteen minutes I was throwing my saddle on the back of another horse, having decided I'd better go look for him before it got dark or the weather got any worse. But as I was riding out the gate in a swirl of snow, I saw him coming down the fence, so I rode back inside the corral and unsaddled my horse. I was leaning on the door facing the saddle house rolling a smoke when he rode in the corral with his horse snorting at Plato's carcass.

"It's about damn time . . ." But it wasn't Josh. It was the lady from Endee! "Lillie Johnson?" I said. "What are *you* doin' here?"

She was wearing a tan riding skirt and only a light coat, and she had nothing on her head or hands. She was cold. Her lips were purple and her face was white. Her black hair was covered with snow, and she was shivering.

"Better get off and come in the house," I said as I dropped the cigarette and took hold of her reins. "You're about to freeze."

I put a chair up close to the stove and threw in a few more chunks of wood. The coffee was still hot, so I poured a cup and held it out to her. She opened and closed her hands slowly.

"I don't think I can hold it yet," she said, and she was still shaking.

"Let's get those wet boots off," I said as I squatted down in front of her and began unlacing them. As soon as I slipped them off, I pulled the other chair in front of her and put her feet on the seat. I felt her stockings—they were wet.

Her face changed from the white it had been when she came into the house to beet red.

"Let's see your fingers," I said. She laid them in the palms of my hands and I looked at them.

"Now pull your hair back from your ears," I said and looked at them, too. "I don't think you've frostbit anything," I said. "Take your coat off and try this coffee again."

When she began sipping from the cup I said, "Now where in the world were you going?"

"I was coming here, Mr. Wills. It wasn't snowing when I left Endee, and it didn't feel very cold."

"There's no Mr. Wills here, just Casey. . . . What in the world were you coming to Trujillo Camp for? You didn't come to collect your two cents, I hope."

"No. . . . I came to tell you about your friend."

"My friend? . . . Josh?"

"Yes. . . . He said he lived at Trujillo Camp."

"What about 'im?" I asked. "Where'd you see 'im?"

"He came to Endee this morning and—"

"Josh was in Endee? What for?"

"Well . . . I don't really know. His face was all skinned up and he acted kind of hurt, but he didn't say much. Just went to the bar and ordered a shot of whiskey."

"Uh-oh," I said.

"After he drank that shot, and a couple of others, he started talking."

I grinned. "Whiskey has a way of thawin' out Josh's tongue."

Now Lillie Johnson grinned. "He said the reason he was so skinned up was because a bunch of outlaws jumped him."

"Good gawd," I said.

"But he said he fought them all off and saved the ranch."

"I'd like to've seen that! Where's he at now?"

"Well . . . he bought a bottle of whiskey and checked into a room—"

"But he didn't have any money," I said. Then I remembered that he *might* have had some money. I lifted the lid from the Arbuckles coffee can. It was empty. "I don't think I need to ask," I said, knowing Josh's brain and elbow worked just opposite of each other—the more his elbow bent, the less his brain worked—"but since you rode all the way out here to tell me I will. . . . And *then* what happened?"

"Well . . . I heard him coughing in his room, and got worried about him. I had Mr. Franks go up and check on him, but your friend threw a chair at him and pulled his gun. Later, I heard him coughing again, only this time not very loud—and he was moaning, too. I decided *I'd* better check on him, so I peeked in his room. He was lying on the floor holding the empty bottle. . . . I knew he might have just been passed out, but he looked terrible."

"Yeah," I said, "I know how scary Josh can look when he passes out on a hotel room floor. . . . So you rode all the way over here to tell me?"

"We didn't know for sure whether he was just drunk or sick. If he was just drunk we didn't know what he would be like when he slept the whiskey off, and if he was really sick we thought you ought to know. I ride a lot anyway and am always looking for some excuse to get away from Endee. At that time the weather wasn't bad, of course. It just started snowing on me four or five miles back, but it wasn't very heavy and I thought I could get on over here and then get back to Endee."

"Thanks for comin' out," I said, "but you should've turned back as soon as it started snowin'. . . . You stay in here and dry your feet and get warm while I go saddle a horse. When I'm ready I'll lead your horse up to the house." I untied my neckerchief and handed it to her. "Better tie this around your ears. I'll see if I can find you some gloves—if I can't you can wear mine."

"Oh please, Casey," she said, "I don't think I can stand to ride in that weather anymore today."

"But I've got to get you home—your people will be

worried about you. We'll hit a long trot, and the wind will be at our backs. . . . You'll make it okay."

"But my toes are *still* numb."

I opened the door and grinned at her. "The feelin' will come back in 'em by the time I get my horse saddled, Mrs. Johnson."

"Lillie," she said. She looked up at me with dark eyes, pulling her hair back with both hands and tilting her head toward the stove.

"Okay . . . Lillie. Stay in here by the stove until I holler at you."

As soon as I stepped outside I was blinded by powdery snow that was being whipped and whirled over and around the house like blow sand by the howling wind. Even from the corner of the house, the barn was only a dim object without outline. In some places the ground was swept clean, but in other places, like in front of the saddle house and the south side of Plato's carcass, drifts were forming.

Standing in the saddle house door, I could barely see the horses in the other pen, with their heads down and their rumps to the wind. Their backs were all white, and their tails were being driven between their hind legs. I caught one and turned the rest out. Outside they could survive nearly anything; inside, if the wind and snow stayed as it was, they could suffocate.

Right then I changed my plans. I unsaddled Lillie's horse and put him and the one I'd just caught inside the barn.

I stepped inside the house and closed the door against the swirling snow. "We're not goin' anywhere right now, Lillie," I said as I stomped the snow off my boots. "We'll go as soon as the snow lets up or the wind dies down. That may be in the next few minutes, or it may not be until tomorrow."

"I guess I shouldn't have come," she said.

"No, you shouldn't have—not in this weather. But you're safe now. I'll make some more coffee and we'll set 'er out. Storms don't last forever, and we've got everything we need. . . . And don't worry about me— I'm harmless."

"Are you sure?" she asked with a bright smile and flashing eyes.

I smiled as I took off my coat. "Sure I am. . . . Josh says the only difference between me and a lazy old dog is the lazy old dog's charm."

Lillie smiled again. . . . And God, how Lillie could smile!

CHAPTER
10

We sat at the table, looking through the window and watching the snow as the day grew steadily darker. We were waiting for the coffee to come to a boil when Lillie asked, "Are you worried about him?"

"Josh?" I answered. "Naw, not really—not since I know he's not lyin' out somewhere with the snow piling up around him. This morning he got his foot hung in the stirrup and wound up underneath a horse—that's how he got all skinned up, *not* fighting a bunch of outlaws and saving the ranch. It looked pretty bad for a while, and I had to kill the horse he was hung to. I know he was all sored up and feelin' bad, not just from getting stomped and kicked but from me killing the horse, too. No cowboy likes to see a horse get killed, not even one as owl-headed as the one he was hung to, and I guess he's blaming himself. He probably went to Endee just to have a couple of drinks, but they went down so easy he decided to have a couple more, and those two went down even easier

84

than the first two did, and . . . " I shrugged my shoulders and lit the lantern on the table.

"Was it his fault that you had to kill the horse?"

"Not really," I said, settling the globe down over a small coal oil flame. "Not unless you can fault a man for gettin' older and not being able to do everything he used to do. Josh will be all right, at least this time. As soon as he sleeps the whiskey off, he'll be back out here blaming everything on me."

"It doesn't sound like you two get along very well."

"Get along?" I chuckled. *"Nobody* gets along with Josh . . . not unless they love him." I shook my head. "Now you see what you've made me do, Lillie? . . . You've already made me say something stupid. If you ever repeat what I just said to *anybody,* I'll . . . I'll never pay you those two cents I owe you."

"My lips are sealed," Lillie said with a smile. Then she got up and walked to the window in her stocking feet and looked out. "I never dreamed it would snow like this. I really shouldn't have come."

"If you hadn't, I'd be out there lookin' for Josh now—so I'm glad you did," I said. "Besides, everybody needs company on a stormy night, and your face is sure a welcome change from Josh's. So I'm glad you're here, Lillie, even if you shouldn't have come. . . . Now, I'm going to whip us up a little supper."

As the tin on the roof banged in the wind and we ate beans and salt pork a little later, I said, "Where'd you live back east?"

"New York," she said.

"I've heard of it. It's east of the XIT, right?"

"Yes," Lillie said with a smile, "it *is* east of the XIT. You should come see it sometime."

"They have any big cow outfits there?"

"They have dairies and stock farms."

"Whew," I said, lifting my eyebrows. "Sounds like my kind of country."

Lillie laughed.

"When are you going back?" I asked.

"I don't know. Someday maybe—if I ever have the money."

"I figured you had money, Lillie."

"No—no money, Casey."

"What about your husband?"

"My hus—? Oh, he was a bookkeeper in a bank, but he didn't have any money either."

"What killed him?"

"They said it was the fever."

I nodded. "What'll you do when you go back?"

Her face lit up. "I want to go to acting school and be in the theater. . . . I guess that sounds foolish to you."

"Not to me, it don't, Lillie, not if that's what you really want to do."

"Is this what you want to do, Casey—be a cow-boy?"

"Oh . . . yeah, sure. I don't reckon I could be anything else."

"It must be a lot of fun—dashing across the prairie chasing buffalo and fighting Indians with your mustang's mane blowing free in the air."

This time I laughed. "Sounds like you're promotin' a Wild West show. . . . I can't say I haven't had my share of fun or that I haven't dashed across the prairie a few times. But I haven't seen five head of buffalo in the last three years, and the only Indians I know of that aren't on a reservation are a few hidin' out in the rocks of Arizona and Mexico. And I haven't seen more than a handful of mustangs in my life that I wouldn't have rather walked and carried my saddle than ride them."

"Then it's *not* all adventure and romance, huh?"

"Oh, there's that," I said, pushing my empty plate back and reaching inside a vest pocket for my sack of Bull Durham, "but sometimes there's more adventure and romance in the tellin' of some story than there is in livin' it. A long time from now, if I live that long, and I'm tellin' about the time me and Josh lived at a camp on the XIT, it might sound plumb thrillin'. But right now there doesn't seem to be much excitement in ridin' fence and greasin' windmills."

"Casey . . . ," Lillie said. She had a strange look on her face that was some puzzling to me. "I'm not as naive about cowboys as I pretended." She looked down and rubbed a finger on the edge of the table. "I've been out here long enough to . . . to've known a few. But you're"—she looked up at me—"you're different."

"I don't think so," I said in all honesty. "We're pretty much alike. Maybe you're used to seein' cowboys in town when they're fresh instead of at a cow camp with the edge off. You see, I figure cowboys are like horses, and nearly any horse is different after you've trotted him around enough to make him break a sweat and take the edge off 'im than he is when he's fresh."

"Okay," Lillie said, "so it's trotting a horse around that takes the edge off him—what takes the edge off cowboys?"

I smiled. "With most of us, cheap whiskey's been known to work wonders."

"And what about you, Casey?"

"Whiskey's been known to work for me, too. . . . But tonight I think it's being alone with a decent woman at a line camp and just talkin'. But I've talked too much. . . . I want to hear *you* talk awhile, Lillie. I want to know—"

Lillie stood up and walked to the window, where ice had formed on the inside and snow had packed on the outside.

"No," she said, keeping her back to me. "I . . . I *really* shouldn't be here. It's already getting dark."

"Well, whether you shouldn't be or not, I'm afraid you're stuck here for the rest of the night anyway. But quit worryin'. Like I said, you're safe in here—there's plenty of wood, and the wind's not going to blow this shack over, in spite of how it sounds. I'll try to get you back to Endee first thing in the mornin'." Then I went into the east room and pulled Josh's bedroll into the west room, putting it beside the stove. "You'll be warmer sleepin' in here by the fire. You can close the door between the rooms and even prop a chair up against it if you want to. I just hope you don't want me to go sleep in the barn."

When she turned around she looked sad in a way, but just the same she was smiling. "Don't be silly, Casey. I didn't mean to imply that you . . . Oh, anyway, this is just fine—with you in one room and me in another. Thank you. And I'm not going to prop a chair against the door."

"Okay," I said. "Just blow out the lantern whenever you're ready. If you hear me up during the night,

I'll just be puttin' more wood in the stove. 'Night, Lillie."

"Good night, Casey," she said.

I lay in the dark in my bedroll for a long time thinking about the woman in the other room. When my eyes were open I saw nothing but the blackness in the room, but whenever I shut them I saw Lillie's face. It wasn't that her face was a bad thing to see, of course, but it was impossible to fall asleep with it so vivid in my mind's eye.

I knew Lillie wasn't the most beautiful woman in the world. She wasn't even the most beautiful woman a cowboy like myself had ever seen. Oh, she *did* have beautiful eyes, so dark and soft. And I always liked a slim face with high cheekbones and full lips like Lillie had. But she had a few lines on her neck, and a few gray hairs among the black on her head. And her teeth weren't perfect—the bottom front ones were a little too crowded together, and the right corner tooth on top was at a slight angle. And her nose was maybe just a little longer than an artist would have given her on canvas.

But, while Lillie's imperfections might have taken away from her on canvas, in real life, especially real life in a big, lonesome country, those imperfections only added something to her that a woman of perfect beauty would have lacked, just like the scars she wore did—the invisible, silent scars of heartache that I had already seen in her dark eyes a couple of times that night.

Slowly, Lillie's face withdrew further and further into the darkness until it disappeared and was replaced by what had happened when the day had begun. Again, I felt the fear I'd known when Josh was hung to Plato and I thought he might be killed. And I felt the Colt jump back and up in recoil as Plato fell. And then I heard me say again, "Nice damn wreck, Josh." And then I guess I fell asleep.

CHAPTER
11

When I peeked out my window and looked toward the southeastern horizon, which was miles and miles away where the breaks fell away from the caprock, I saw faint streaks of soft orange against a sky that was still dark and filled with a million twinkling stars. The snow was over, and I was surprised at how little was on the ground. Had all of it fallen straight down, the ground would have probably been covered by a couple of inches, but no more than that. As it was, the wind had swept large areas around the house and barn clean of any snow at all. In other places there were drifts, but the deepest of them was probably less than a foot deep. We had hardly been in the grip of a raging blizzard all night. In fact, it looked like it must have stopped snowing completely right after dark.

I put on my boots, coat and hat without waking Lillie and then slipped outside to do the chores and chop some more firewood. It was cold outside, as it always is on a clear morning following a snow, but there was a slight breeze from the southwest, which meant warmer temperatures after a while.

Back in the house, I heated some water and shaved and then drank a half a pot of coffee while Lillie slept and day broke outside. I knew I could have gotten her back to Endee last night before midnight with no trouble and felt sort of guilty for not having done so. But then, as I got up to start breakfast and looked down at her sleeping on her side in Josh's bedroll with both hands underneath her face and the black hair pulled back from her ear, I wasn't sorry about it any longer.

I cut a long strip of loin off the side of beef hanging on the north side of the house and was frying it in a skillet when I glanced down at Lillie again and saw her looking up at me.

"Mornin'," I said. "Do you remember where you are?"

She stretched and smiled. "I remember. Ummmm, that smells good." Then she sat up in Josh's bedroll, and I handed a cup of coffee to her. "Were you able to sleep?"

She took a sip of coffee. "Oh . . . that's good. I slept wonderful." She stood up, set her cup on the table and straightened her clothes. "I'm not sure I woke up even one time. . . . Oh, look how bright and clear it is outside!"

"Yeah, it's clear as a bell. . . . You were probably so tired you could have slept on a pallet of rocks."

"I guess I *was* tired, Casey." She sat down at the table and cradled the coffee cup in both hands. "And it felt so comfortable and warm in here, especially listening to the wind howling outside. After I blew out the lantern and lay down I felt so relaxed and safe. . . ."

"Then the Trujillo Hotel's not so bad, huh? In spite of the furnishings *and* the cook?"

"It's just about the nicest hotel I've ever stayed in," she said. "It's comfortable, the furnishings are quaint, and the chef is—"

"Bowlegged," I said, flipping over the slice of loin.

She laughed. "Oh, Casey. . . . It's really been fun."

With her seeming so happy and looking so bright and pretty, that bowlegged cow waddie standing at the stove with the shotgunned boots and spurs, wearing the white shirt buttoned at the throat, had hardly a care in the whole wide world. When I looked at Lillie Johnson, it was as if I'd never looked at another woman in my life, never really *seen* another woman.

Of course, I tried not to let what I was feeling show in any way, and I sure couldn't talk about it. But I felt like I had to say something, so I said, "I'll have you back to Endee by ten o'clock."

Lillie looked sort of disappointed. "I know you're ready to get rid of me, Casey. And I know you want to see about Josh, but . . ." Her face began to light up again. "Have you seen the Blue Hole? It's a spring just a few miles from here in New Mexico in Rana Canyon. It's *real* deep and blue and pretty and . . ."

"Maybe we could ride by it on the way to Endee then," I said.

Lillie's eyes lit up even more. *"Could* we?"

I shrugged my shoulders, trying to act at least partially disinterested, but chances are my eyes gave me away. "Well," I said, "if you can find this Blue Hole and it's not but a few miles out of the way, I don't see why we couldn't. It looks like it's going to warm up pretty good and—"

"Do you think we could fry some extra beef and take it with us?"

"Sure. . . . And I'll put a coffeepot in a sack with the beef," I said.

"Casey . . . this sounds like a picnic to me."

"Sounds like it to me, too," I said.

The Blue Hole turned out to be seven or eight miles northwest of Trujillo Camp, but the country in between was open, sandy country where a horse could strike a jig of a trot and stay in it for miles. On top of that, even though the sun had started to melt the snow before we rode out of Trujillo Camp, it was still the kind of a chilly morning when a jig of a trot, the kind that keeps your blood from settling to the bottom and getting thick and cold, felt good.

So the ride from Trujillo to the edge of a deep, deep hole fifty feet across and filled with sky blue spring water hidden in the bottom of a pretty little rocky canyon turned out to be nothing more and nothing less than *the* perfect ride to make a hot cup of coffee sound good, especially one fresh-boiled over an open fire.

The Blue Hole was as pretty a place as I'd ever seen, and not *just* pretty either, but cowboy pretty, too. That little canyon had about everything a cowboy would have ordered if he'd been given an order form from God to mark what all he wanted to put in his heaven. It had protection from blizzards, and it had grass and water and cottonwood trees and rocks and rimrocks and rimrock cedars. And it even had a little deserted rock cabin no more than a stone's throw from the spring that a man could have had livable in short order.

As I squatted down on my spurs beside the fire waiting for the coffee to come to a boil, I looked up and down that canyon, taking in the beauty of it, and then I looked across the fire at Lillie, sitting on the ground hugging her knees with black hair flowing down her back and a small strand of it catching a breeze and being laid across her soft cheek. In the reflection in her dark eyes I saw the smoke rising from the fire and I saw the rock cabin beside the spring, and I saw . . .

. . . *a man coming off the rimrock. He looked like he had been in the saddle a long time. He was hot and tired as he rounded a bend in the canyon and saw the rock cabin, a column of smoke rising from its stovepipe. Approaching, he caught the smell of cedar smoke and baking bread. He saw the breeze stir the drying wash on the line, the curtains on the windows, and he saw it gently stir the soft, dark hair of the pretty woman coming out the narrow door to meet him, wiping her hands on her apron and smiling . . .*

"Casey? . . . Casey, don't you want to eat?"

"What? . . . Yeah . . . sure," I said as I reached out and took a strip of fried beef from her.

"What were you thinking about just now?"

"Oh . . . nothin' that matters," I said. "You're right about this place, Lillie—it *is* pretty. Of course, to you it probably seems like a terribly lonesome place."

"Casey"—Lillie lay back in the winter grass with her head turned toward me—"right now it doesn't seem lonesome at all. . . . I was looking at that house and thinking . . ." Then a sudden change seemed to come over her like a dark cloud crossing in front of the sun and putting gloomy shadows over what had a minute ago been bright and sunny.

"Lookin' at the house and thinkin' what?" I asked.

She paused a long time. Then she stood up and said, "I was thinking it was time I was getting back to where I belonged."

It was not a short trot on to Endee, but during all that time Lillie spoke not a single word. By the time we stopped at the top of the ridge about a half mile north of our destination, the winter sun was no more than four fingers off the southwestern horizon and the temperature was dropping fast.

Our horses were standing quietly side by side, glad for the chance to rest. I reached over and touched the back of Lillie's hand, the only time I'd touched her at all except for when I'd unlaced her wet boots at Trujillo Camp.

"Lillie . . . ," I said.

"Don't, Casey," she said, looking straight ahead and pulling her hand away. "Don't." Then she kicked her horse into a lope, toward Endee—toward the two-story building standing alone on the other side of the draw.

I caught up with her just as she was getting off her horse in front of the hotel. "Lillie!" I said, and out of the corner of my eye I saw Josh's horse. He was still there! Lillie was tying her horse to the rail. "Lillie, what—"

Then I looked up on the porch and there stood who else in all the world but George Findlay, the XIT bookkeeper. Standing beside Findlay was a tall man wearing shotgunned boots and spurs and leggin's. And he had on a hat, a real hat, not one of the stupid, narrow-brimmed kind like Findlay wore that didn't look like a hat at all.

"Hello, Wills," Findlay said as he and the other man looked first at me and then at Lillie, who by then was going through the door that the other man, the cowboy kind of man, was holding open for her. "This is Troy Greg, the new boss of the Alamocitas Division. . . . Troy, this is Casey Wills, the *other* man staying at Trujillo Camp."

I thought, Uh-oh.

I've never seen a cowboss who didn't have miserable timing when it came to observing his cowboys at work, so I don't know why I should have been so disappointed that our new boss didn't catch me and Josh greasin' windmills, or skinnin' out dead cattle, or repairin' fence, or paintin' the barn, or drivin' cattle off from a dry water hole, or any of the things we'd done every day since we'd been at Trujillo Camp but that particular day.

I'll be the first to admit that what Findlay and Greg *had* seen that day at Trujillo Camp and at Endee, not knowing and understanding all the particulars and extenuating circumstances, was not likely to exactly endear management to labor.

"Wills," Greg said, "we got to Trujillo this mornin' and found a dead company horse and an empty whiskey bottle layin' beside 'im in front of the saddle house. Then we come along the fence toward Endee and we find two places where the fence has been cut and pulled back and cattle obviously driven through." Nothing Greg said surprised me except for this, and this not only surprised me but made me feel . . . it made me feel like I think I would've felt if I'd watched my mother drown in a river while I sat on the bank and fished, or if I'd played cards while my sisters were all being violated.

"Then," Greg went on, "then we get *here* and find one of the hands passed out in a hotel room, and the other one comes ridin' in wearin' a clean white shirt and chasin' a woman. . . . Now if *you* were the boss, Wills, just how in the hell would you handle this?"

"Well, Mr. Greg," I said, pushing my hat back with a thumb and then resting both hands on the saddle horn, "here's what I'd do: I'd say, 'Boys, now I know there's a damn good explanation for all of this, so let's just sit down and you can explain it all to me. Afterward, I'll get on my horse and ride back to headquarters and let you boys take care of the ranch while I try to get you both a raise in wages.'"

I wasn't trying to be a smart aleck and I wasn't as nonchalant as I might have sounded. But my cowboy pride was wounded, and I could see the writing on the wall, having seen other writings on other walls a time or two before. I knew that I'd have as much luck reviving old Plato as I would successfully pleading my and Josh's case before a pair of judges whose minds were already made up and whose gavels were already on the way down to pronounce the case closed.

Findlay didn't smile at what I'd said, but Greg did, and I appreciated that. I always appreciated a man who could smile and fire me at the same time. "Wills," he said, "you and Smith'd just as well to roll your beds. I'll leave it up to you to tell him and to get all your stuff outa the camp by sundown tomorrow. The money both of you have comin' together should just about cover the dead horse." Then Greg stopped smiling and got serious. "I'd have probably been able to overlook everything else this time, Wills, but it's hard to overlook the fact that one of you was drunk and the other was off galin' while cattle were being stolen from the outfit."

"I'm sorry it came to this, Wills," Findlay said, "but having personally witnessed yours and Smith's total lack of respect for authority and failure to adhere to any sort of acceptable work ethic, I think it was inevitable. We are making sweeping changes on the XIT—progressive changes, such as spelling out in black and white what sort of conduct will and will not be tolerated on the ranch. The old general manager, Campbell, is gone and so is Billy Nye and nearly a hundred other cowboys. We are—"

"Mr. Findlay," I said, tired of listening to him, "me and Josh have both been fired from better outfits than this one without havin' to listen to a bunch of nonsensical bullshit from someone who couldn't find his way to the barn from the back side of the water lot."

I stepped off my horse, wrapped a rein around the rail and stepped up on the porch. "Mr. Greg," I said, "me 'n Josh are fired, and I'll accept that. I want you to know that I don't apologize for killin' that horse because he would've probably killed Josh if I hadn't. He hurt Josh some as it was—that's why Josh is here now. I ain't apologizin' or makin' excuses for him—if he wants to do that he can do it himself—that's just the way it is. But goddammit . . . I *shoulda* rode that fence early this mornin'."

Greg nodded to me. Although I'd just been fired by him, we had a kinship of sorts that somebody like Findlay could never understand.

"Mr. Wills," Findlay said as I stepped toward the door, "you should be aware that rule number three of the new General Rules of XIT Ranch states that employees discharged or leaving the service of the company are expected to leave the ranch at once and will not be permitted to remain—"

"George," Greg said, "why don't you get on your horse and shut up?"

CHAPTER
12

Despite its many and varied attractions, Endee was not fast becoming one of this cowboy's favorite in-the-middle-of-nowhere towns. I had spent no more than a total of fifteen minutes there in two separate visits, but they were sure not fifteen dull and boring minutes, at least there was that to say for Endee. For during that time I had suffered the indignity of having a hole shot in the ear of the horse I had underneath me at the time and, now, of being fired from the largest ranch in the world, at least under fence.

In my past, and when in the proper frame of mind, I had been known to step up to a long bar and make a considerable investment in cheap whiskey. I was in that exact frame of mind when I stepped inside the hotel at Endee and observed the long bar along the north wall, and I believe the transaction could have gone off without a hitch if I had had the capital to invest. But I had none. In over five months of working for the largest ranch in the world—*under fence*—I had felt the reassuring tug of cash in my pocket only once, that being the ride from Alamocitas Camp to Tascosa the afternoon the fall wagon had pulled in. As famous as the XIT was, it was hard to see how I had benefited from our association in any way.

So I merely looked longingly at the bar as I walked across the floor of Endee's hotel, by her post office and through her general store on my way upstairs to see Josh. Then I remembered rumor had it that he—Josh —had made a recent investment of the type I had been thinking about. An investment no doubt made with funds withdrawn from the Arbuckles can that was all marked to go back to Tatum Stagg.

When I opened the door to room number 212, it was easy to see the rumors had been correct. It was also easy to see, considering the price of the room and the two empty bottles of whiskey on the floor, that a goodly amount of the money from the Arbuckles can had *not* gotten back into Tatum Stagg's charitable hands.

"Josh!" He was on the bed asleep. "I'd have bet anything you'd have been back to Trujillo first thing this mornin' . . . Josh?" I shook the foot of the bed, and he turned his head toward me. He looked bad. "Are you still on the neck oil?" I asked.

"I ain't drunk, Casey," he said softly. "At least I ain't anymore."

I stepped closer to the bed. "Then what in the hell are you?"

"I'm sick," he moaned. "I'm a sick bastard, Casey."

I looked at the empty whiskey bottles on the floor again and said, "You *oughta* be a sick bastard."

"It ain't—" He coughed—weak, like a sick calf. "It ain't that kinda sick, Casey. . . . Maybe somethin' old

Plato done to my innards. Or maybe somethin' else. . . . Just get me back to Trujillo, Casey. I don't want to die in here."

"Good gawd, Josh!" I said. "If you died ever' time you said you were going to after a drunk I'd a spent half of the last ten years diggin' graves for you." I jerked the covers off him in an unsympathetic, playful mood, but when those covers came off I was shocked at how old and pale he looked. Then I saw a little blood smeared on the sheet where he'd been wiping his mouth. "Damn, Josh," I said.

"Not so goddamn smart now, are you?" he said and tried to smile. He had a short coughing spell and then said in a breathless voice that was almost a whisper, "Get me outa here, Casey. . . . Help me down the stairs and on my horse and I can make it to Trujillo. I'll be okay once we get home."

A cowboy calls anywhere he unrolls his bed more than a couple of times "home." I didn't want to tell him Trujillo Camp wouldn't be *our* home anymore, not with him as sick as he looked. I reached over and felt his forehead. "I don't think so, Josh. You've got a fever. You'd better stay here tonight."

"But what about the chores—and we gotta drag Plato outa the pens. And we gotta push them cows away from that mudhole in Mohair Creek before they start boggin' down. You rode the fence this mornin', didn't you? I was gonna go home this mornin' and ride it from this way, but—"

"Dammit, Josh," I said. "Quit worryin' about what needs doin'. I'll go home and take care of things and come back and get you in the mornin'. . . . It won't hurt to spend a little more of Stagg's money. Where is it?"

Josh reached under his pillow and pulled out a roll of bills and handed the roll to me.

"Why . . . it's all here," I said as I counted the money out on the bed. "All hundred and twenty dollars. How did you pay for the whiskey and the room?"

Josh started coughing again, and coughing bad. I put the money in my pocket, backed quietly out of the room, went downstairs and outside onto the porch. Lillie was sitting out there alone. She looked up at me with a sad face and red-rimmed eyes.

"Lillie? What's wrong? Why are you out here by yourself in the cold?"

"I heard what your bosses said, Casey," she answered. "I'm sorry. It's all my fault. I . . ."

I buttoned my coat and looked down at her. "It's not your fault, Lillie. You didn't make Josh get hurt, or sick, *or* drunk. And you didn't hold a gun on me and make me ride to Rana Canyon instead of comin' back to Endee along the fence like I knew I should have."

"No, Casey, but—"

"Lillie . . . I'm leavin' right now for Tascosa. I'm going to find a doctor and bring him back here to look at Josh."

"Why? What's wrong with him? I thought he was just drunk."

"I'm sure he *was,* but that's not what's wrong with him now. He's coughin' and has a fever. I'll get back as soon as I can with a doctor, but until I do I wonder if you would look in on him now and then. . . . And *don't* tell him that we don't have a job anymore, or that me and you came back here without ridin' the fence. I'll be back as soon as I can, but it's about sixty miles one way. If I ride all night I'll get to Tascosa by daylight, and try to be back here by sundown tomorrow."

"I'll take care of Josh for you, Casey," Lillie said, standing now in front of me. "And I really am sorry about all of this. . . . I can't tell you how sorry I am."

I stepped closer to her and put a hand underneath her chin and lifted her face up. I leaned over her, smelling her perfume and the sweetness of her breath at the same time. "Lillie . . . can I kiss you?" I whispered. She didn't answer, but she closed her eyes and didn't pull away.

So I kissed her.

Lillie's lips were soft and warm against mine—and she was kissing me back!

I put my arms around her and pulled her body against mine until I could feel the softness and warmth of her breasts even through our clothes.

My heart was beating wilder than I'd ever felt it before, even the times when I thought I was in danger. My brain was numb, but my body was alive and tingling with excitement.

After a few seconds our lips slowly came apart and Lillie laid her head on my chest.

"Oh . . . Lillie," I whispered, taking in the aroma of her and feeling the softness of her hair against my face. "Lillie, I—"

"Don't say anything, Casey," she said softly. "Just hold me in your arms."

In a few seconds she said, "Now go to Tascosa and get the doctor."

Luckily there was a three-quarter Texas moon that night and only a few clouds. That meant it was cold—skim ice started forming on the tanks at windmills even before sundown—but it also meant there was plenty of light by which to travel. I put the XIT horse I was on in a long trot on a slack rein, pulled my weight forward in the saddle and plotted a northeastward course in my head, keeping in mind the two fences I would have to cross and where the gates in them were.

Fences and gates and trails across creeks and canyons weren't all I had on my mind that night, and the course between Endee and Tascosa was not all I was plotting either. There had been a lot happened in a short time, and I was thinking about all of it: . . . Josh . . . Plato . . . being fired. And then there was Lillie, so sweet and fresh and innocent, and the way she looked, the way she walked, the way she talked, the way she smiled, the way she felt in my arms, the way her breath smelled, the way her lips tasted. I plotted to have her. I *had* to have her.

I wanted more than to "have" her in the Biblical sense, although, with her sweet taste still fresh on my lips and the feel of her body pressing against mine chiseled deep in my brain, I desired her passionately. But I meant to do right by Lillie. I meant to marry Lillie, and most of the plotting I did as I rode to Tascosa was how to make a life together possible for us.

I even had a plan! Or at least I was in the process of drawing one up. *Me,* Casey Wills, the drifting drifter of short stays and long trails, whose planning for the future had always before meant nothing more than making decisions about which horse to catch for the next morning's circle, was now making *lifelong* plans which included settling down and having a home, marrying Lillie, raising kids with her and building a place for all of us. It was the first time in my life I had ever been hit by such notions, but they'd hit me hard and had me reeling.

I couldn't wait to tell Josh about me and Lillie and our future and how we'd always keep a plate set at the supper table for him. I wasn't going to tell him just yet, but I had already decided to name our first son after him, too. *Our* first son, that's the way I thought about it. One thing about a pretty woman's kiss and its lingering aftereffects that a cowboy would do well to remember is that as passion increases, logic decreases—if a man is plumb full of passion, then he is also plumb out of logic.

CHAPTER

13

Sometime during the very earliest hours of the morning, after having ridden some forty-odd miles, most of it in a long trot, I came to Alamocitas Camp, the headquarters of the whole XIT, and there exchanged one used-up XIT horse for one fresh XIT horse without waking anyone. Highly expedient and hardly stealing. George Findlay, however, would no doubt have had trouble with the fact that I was on *any* kind of XIT horse at all. Therefore, I felt it was only doing him a great kindness to handle the exchange as quietly and discreetly as possible.

The sun came up over Tascosa's eastern horizon just about the same time I came up over her western horizon, and together the sun and I woke Dr. Merriam. When he came to the door in his nightshirt, he did not seem thrilled to see either of us.

"You're needed at Endee, Doc," I said.

"Good grief, mister," he said, "I couldn't possibly go all the way to Endee."

"I'll pay you twenty dollars cash," I told him.

"It's not a matter of money," Dr. Merriam explained. "I just have too many patients to see here today."

"Twenty-five," I said.

"Look . . . I *told* you it is *not* a matter of money!"

"Thirty."

"Well . . ." I could see the compassion rising in his eyes. Then he shook his head and waved me off with a hand. "No. . . . It would just not be possible."

"Thirty-five," I said, cocking my head. "And that's final."

"You know, today's not the day I thought it was after all. . . . Give me ten minutes."

As Dr. Merriam and I were riding out of town by way of Main Street, I heard someone yell my name. "Casey . . . *Casey!*"

I pulled up and started looking. My eyes finally came to rest on the pole corral built onto the west side of McCormick's Livery, which was a block behind me. There were two men and several horses inside the corral. One of the men was leaning against the fence and the other was standing on the second pole. I squinted my eyes against the just-up sun to get a better look.

"Casey!" the man perched on the corral pole said again. This time I recognized the voice coming from the form outlined against the glare of the sun. Wearing a grin, I reined my horse around in the street and trotted back to the livery.

"Hello, Casey," Johnnie Lester said, as we leaned toward each other to shake hands.

Ab Deacons was the man on the ground, and he too stepped up on the second pole, leaned over and extended his hand. "Good to see ya again, Casey," he said with a strong handshake. "We thought you were goin' to ride right out of town without sayin' hello."

"I figured, being an employed person on the largest ranch in the world, you couldn't hardly lower yourself to associate with prairie urchins and riffraff with no visible means of support," Johnnie teased.

I grinned and winked at Ab. "No, it wasn't that so much, Johnnie. . . . I just didn't recognize you here in town with your clothes on." I looked at the milling dozen or so horses in the pen. "I figured y'all would be in Montana or somewhere by now."

"Naw," Johnnie said, "Montana's too damn cold this time of year."

"So you found work here, huh?"

They both laughed. "We found plenty of goddamn *work* all right, Casey, but no job like you an' Josh got. We've helped build a set of brandin' pens for the LX and we've scooped mud out of a couple of drinkin' tubs for old man McMasters."

"What're you doin' in town?" Johnnie asked. "Where's Josh? Heard y'all were at Trujillo Camp."

"Me an' Josh have left the service of the company," I said.

They both widened their eyes and laughed. "What? Already! . . . You get fired or quit?"

"Well," I said slowly, nodding my head, "we was asked to roll our beds."

"You just barely had time to get settled at Trujillo," Ab said. "What the hell happened?"

"Aw, hell," I said, "not much. They let Billy Nye go, and a feller named Troy Greg took his place—not a bad kind of a feller, I don't think, not really. Anyway, Findlay brought him out to Trujillo yesterday, and I guess they didn't much like what they saw."

"So where's Josh? Where are y'all goin'?" Johnnie said.

"Josh is in Endee, boys," I answered. "I came to get Doc Merriam to go see about him."

"What's wrong with 'im, Casey?"

"Don't know for sure. He got stomped pretty good day before yesterday, and after that he drank a lot of whiskey. Now he's sicker 'n hell, and I don't know for sure what's wrong."

"He ain't bad enough to die or anything, is he?" Ab asked.

"Naw," I answered, shaking my head, "he's probably just sored up and hung over, but he thinks he's pretty sick."

"You must think so too," Johnnie said, "to come this far to get a doctor."

"Well . . . he *did* look like hell layin' in that hotel room. He looked worse than I've ever seen him."

"We'll be through with these horses in a couple of hours," Johnnie said. "Then we might just trot over to Endee and help you tail the old fart up."

"Good," I said. "I better get the doc over there." I reined my horse around to leave, but just as I did so I had a sudden thought. I pulled up and twisted in the saddle to look back. "Hey . . . I just had a damn thought—why don't y'all go out to Alamocitas and tell 'em you just heard Trujillo Camp was open."

"I don't know," Johnnie said. "I don't know if I can work for that outfit anymore."

Ab said, "It wouldn't bother you and Josh, us takin' a camp y'all just got fired from?"

"No," I said, "hell no. You two probably can't handle it like me an' Josh did, but other than that, it won't bother us. Besides, if y'all are at Trujillo, we'll be neighbors."

"Whadaya mean 'neighbors'?"

"There's the prettiest little canyon in the world just a few miles west of Trujillo with the nicest spring you ever saw in it and a deserted rock cabin right close to the spring. I think I'm goin' to live there, probably even file on it."

They looked at each other and then looked at me.

"Yeah, that's right," I said. "I'm going to file on a homestead and settle down. There's this girl at Endee. . . ." I guess I just had to tell someone what I'd been thinking about all night as I rode toward Tascosa.

"And I'll bet she's as pretty and nice as that spring down in that canyon, huh?" Johnnie said.

I couldn't help but smile. I *wanted* to smile. "She sure as hell is, boys. Her name's Lillie and—"

"Good gawdamightdamn!" Johnnie said, hanging his head for a second and then picking it up again to look at me. "What in the ever-lovin' hell has been goin' on over there? Have you gone plumb crazy, Casey?"

"Don't give me no hell, boys—I know what I want! Just wait till you meet her!"

"What about Josh?"

"He's goin' to be welcome to live with us—me and Lillie. I hope he will."

Dr. Merriam came riding up to me then and said,

"I thought you were in a big hurry to get me to Endee."

"I am, Doc," I said. "Let's go." I looked back at Johnnie and Ab one more time as Merriam and I were trotting away. "See you fellers soon's you get to Endee. Hope Greg hires you."

CHAPTER
14

I would not have cared to punch cows with Dr. Merriam. He sat a horse only slightly better than George Findlay, and he had to stop every three or four miles to stretch his legs, rub his butt, empty his bladder or complain about this or that. He told me it was a good thing for me that he had not remembered just how far it was from Tascosa to Endee or he would never have consented to make the trip, which I knew was doctor talk for saying he wished he had held out for another five bucks.

By the time we got close enough to Endee to see it, it was not a single frame building set alongside a wide and lonesome draw, but a few squares of pale yellow light in the distance that looked smaller and farther away than did the evening star shining brightly in the cold, dim twilight above it.

There were a few people downstairs as Dr. Merriam and I entered. There was a man and his wife and two children sitting at a table and eating, two men playing dominoes, two more at the bar, and Lloyd Franks was behind the bar. Most of the people there were likely homesteaders, for New Mexico—unlike just across the fence in Texas, where one group of men held title to three million acres—was a place that wanted and encouraged homesteaders to file on a quarter section and make themselves a home without having to have the money to buy the land. I glanced around for Lillie but didn't see her, so I led Dr. Merriam up the stairs to Josh's room.

I pushed open the door to room 212. The lantern on the bed stand was burning, and Lillie was there—leaning over Josh, wiping his forehead with a rag.

"How's he doing?" I asked when Lillie turned around, looking clean and fresh and pretty with her hair put in a bun at the back of her head and wearing a light blue gingham suit trimmed in white lace. All at once I remembered how I looked, and I wished I was cleaned up and fresh shaven, but I wasn't, and the best I could do along those lines right then was to take my hat off and smooth down my hair with my hand.

Lillie shook her head and whispered, "He's asleep." She stepped over to the doorway where Merriam and I were standing. "Is he the doctor?"

"I'm Dr. Merriam from Tascosa. You look familiar, ma'am—do I know you?"

"I doubt it," Lillie said. And then she looked at Josh and said, "He ate a little something this morning, and I thought he was a little better, but since noon I think his fever has come back up and his cough is worse."

Dr. Merriam moved to the bed and placed his bag on it. As he opened the bag and reached inside it, he said, "Tell me about him. He looks like he's been hurt."

"He got hung to a horse day before yesterday about daylight on a camp about a dozen miles from here," I said, "but I didn't think he was hurt all that bad. After that he rode here and started drinkin' and—"

"How much did he drink?" Dr. Merriam asked as he pulled his stethoscope out of the bag.

"There was two empty whiskey bottles in here the first time I saw him," I said.

"You cowboys never learn moderation, do you? . . . I'd like to do my examination in private, so if you folks would step outside."

"Lillie," I said as soon as we were in the hall. She smelled so good and looked so beautiful and sweet it was all I could do to not reach out and grab her. It wasn't that I didn't care about Josh or the fact that he was sick, but I knew he would be okay; I knew how tough he was. But the promise—the promise of the nights of love and delights in Lillie's arms, but also of the days following those nights when we would build a future together—was on my mind and clawing at my body like a mountain lion on a yearling colt. "Lillie . . . I've been thinking about me and Josh—and you —and what we're goin' to do now. And I've been thinking about that pretty little canyon with the cabin and spring in it where we were yesterday—"

"Please, Casey . . . not now." She started down the hall, saying without looking back, "I've got things to do," then disappeared down the stairs.

I stayed in the hall a few minutes leaning against the wall before I walked to the top of the staircase and looked down. Tatum Stagg was down there, standing with his back to the bar, a boot up on the brass railing. He was talking to Lillie. Their conversation did not seem to be strictly business, like employee to patron, but it did not seem to be strictly social either. When I saw Stagg put his hand on Lillie's arm and her reach up and remove it, I pulled my hat tight on my head and started down the stairs. But at the same time I heard Dr. Merriam open the door to Josh's room. I glanced back downstairs and, seeing Stagg leaving, turned around, went back up and asked Dr. Merriam in the hall, "What do you think, Doc? Too much meat from eatin' my butt out so many times?"

"He's most likely got broken ribs, a ruptured spleen, possibly a punctured lung and other internal injuries."

"Sounds kinda bad," I said, standing up straighter.

"Yeah. . . . They'd be bad enough by themselves, but he's come down with something even worse—pneumonia."

"Good gawd. . . . He ain't gonna . . . die, is he?"

"We're all going to die, Wills—sooner or later. . . . But I would say your friend is in the process now."

"What!" I couldn't believe what he was saying. "But . . . ain't there *something* you can do?"

The doctor shook his head. "I'm afraid nobody can do anything at this point but the good Lord. Your friend might have gotten over the internal injuries in time—if they were all he had. And he might have the strength to fight off the pneumonia, if that was all his body had to contend with. But with both things at the same time . . ." Dr. Merriam shook his head again. "When he came here and drank all that liquor—well, alcohol puts fluid in your system anyway, and he drank himself into such a stupor he couldn't get up, which let most of that fluid settle to his lungs, and *that* fluid, along with the fluid that would naturally accumulate from the internal injuries, caused pneumonia in the one lung that's still inflated—and that is the most direct threat to his life. But, like I said, either one alone and he would most likely pull through. I can't say that he won't anyway, Wills, I'm just telling you like I see it, as honestly as I can."

"I should have stayed with him after Plato stomped him," I said.

Dr. Merriam laid a hand on my shoulder. "There's no need to blame yourself, son. Nobody made him drink that much liquor—sometimes we're our own worst enemy. Is he your father or some relative?"

"No."

"Just"—Dr. Merriam shrugged—"a cowboy?"

"Yeah," I answered. "Yeah . . . he's *just* a cowboy, Dr. Merriam."

Dr. Merriam looked past me, down the hall. I turned my head and saw Lillie going down the stairs again. "She was standing behind you while we were talking," he said. "She's upset, I know. Is she your wife?"

"No . . . not yet anyway."

"She sure is an attractive woman. I'm going to see if I can get a bite to eat downstairs, and then I'll check into a room. I can stay at least until tomorrow morning."

I was sitting on the porch and leaning against the wall smoking a cigarette when Ab and Johnnie came riding up, each leading a packhorse.

"Lucky we found you so quick," Ab said. "You never said which hotel you and Josh were stayin' at."

"This is Ab's first trip to Endee," Johnnie said. "It's easy to see how impressed he is."

"You think this is somethin'," I said. "Just wait'll

118

you see it in the daylight. You boys go by Alamocitas?"

"We did," Johnnie answered. "And we're now gainfully employed. Greg said to kick yours and Josh's ass out of the house and run you off the place if you were still at Trujillo when we got there—that's rule number three of the longest list of rules you ever seen."

"Guess you'll have to kick, then," I told him while I laughed, "'cause we haven't got our stuff out yet."

"You and Josh are nice fellers, you're just irresponsible as hell—at least that's the way me and Findlay and Greg have you figured out," Johnnie volunteered as he and Ab stepped down from their saddles. "What'd the doc say about Josh? Or did Josh cuss him out and run him off before he ever got his bag opened? He didn't hit 'im, did he?"

I sat there on the porch with my arms on my knees and my hands hanging limp for a few seconds while Johnnie and Ab stepped up on the porch. "The doc said . . . He said . . . He said . . . huh . . . Goddammit, Josh probably ain't gonna make it—that's what he said."

We went on up to the room. Josh was awake. "What 'n the hell are you tryin' to pull now, Josh?" Johnnie asked. "I guess you think you're gonna lay in that bed all winter?"

Josh looked pale, but I didn't think he looked as bad as he had earlier, and he was still Josh. "No," he answered. "D'rectly I plan on gettin' up just after Christmas and kickin' your ass like I did at Alamocitas that night. . . . 'Lo, Ab. . . . What 'n the hell are you two doin' here?"

"Hell," Johnnie said, "we're goin' to Trujillo to try and clean up the mess over there. Since you and Casey got fired—"

Josh coughed. "What's he talkin' about, Casey?"

I gave Johnnie a hard look. "Oh, hell, you know how him and Ab are always jokin'."

"We didn't get fired, did we?" he asked.

"Hell no! They can't run that outfit without us and they know it, Josh. Why even Findlay himself said he couldn't believe what we'd done."

"Findlay? When did you see him?"

"Yesterday and—"

"Oh shit. . . . What'd he say about me bein' here—and about Plato bein' dead?"

"All he said was as soon as you could ride, and if we didn't mind, he wanted us to come to headquarters and kill a couple of owl-headed bastards they got there."

We all laughed.

"I thought you was gonna take me home, Casey?"

"In the mornin', Josh," I answered.

"Casey tell you about me gettin' hung to old Plato?"

"Yeah, Josh," Ab answered. "He told us."

"I couldn't get on or off the bastard either one," he said. He started coughing again, and this time he coughed long and hard, until he finally threw up in a bucket I held for him.

"You better get some sleep," I said. "So we can go home tomorrow."

He was whispering again. "I'm gonna die, ain't I, Casey?"

I looked at him and let out a long slow breath. "What the hell do doctors know about cowboys?" I said. I wasn't just saying that as a way to not answer

Josh's question directly, it was what I was really thinking—What the hell *do* doctors know about cowboys?

"Endee, New Mexico," Josh said softly. "Who in the hell would've thought it?" He laughed a little and coughed a little. "It's taken me a long time to get here . . . and it seems like I only left home such a damn short time ago."

It seemed like from then on Josh got steadily worse. His breathing and his coughing got more rattly, and we couldn't put enough blankets on him to keep him from shivering. At eleven o'clock Dr. Merriam came in to check him and left the room looking at me in the dim lantern light and shaking his head. At about one o'clock I was standing beside the bed looking down at him; Johnnie and Ab were both asleep on the floor. Josh opened his eyes and whispered, "She's here."

"Who?" I asked.

Josh looked past me and smiled.

I turned my head and saw Lillie standing silently and nervously in the doorway.

I motioned for her to come in.

Josh raised his hand feebly toward her, his eyes only on her face.

Lillie looked at me. I nodded to her, and she leaned over him.

He touched her hair, rubbed a strand of it between his fingers, pulled it across his face and heavily breathed in the fragrance of it.

When Josh let out that long breath, it was his very last, and on it was carried his last word: "Anna."

CHAPTER
15

The next morning at dawn I paid Dr. Merriam thirty-five dollars in cash from the money Tatum Stagg had left me and Josh. I hated to use any of the money, but it was all I had to carry out my end of the agreement with Merriam. I had already been figuring in my head, though: Josh's two horses should more than cover the thirty-five dollars I had to use to pay Dr. Merriam; if I gave Josh's horses to Stagg, along with the cash I had left, we should be square. But there was still the rent on Josh's room and his whiskey that would have to be paid for. He said he hadn't had to pay for them, but what he meant was "yet," of course.

As soon as Dr. Merriam rode away, we dug a grave for Josh. After the grave was dug we started making Josh's coffin from planks Lloyd Franks let us pull off the lean-to barn built onto the south side of the hotel.

"I think it would've been better if old Plato had've killed him outright, right out there in front of the saddle house at Trujillo Camp—maybe kicked him in the head," I said.

"Hell, that wouldn't a killed him!" Johnnie said. "All that woulda done would've been to knock a hunk outa Plato's hoof."

"It just don't seem like old Josh should've died in a hotel room in Endee—in a room that smelled like stale liquor and death."

"Well," Ab said, "maybe he wasn't smellin' stale liquor and death when he died. Maybe he was smellin' sweet perfume. What did you say he called that woman who was leanin' over him when he died?"

"He called her Anna, but her name's Lillie. *My* Lillie. You boys ain't seen her yet, have you?"

"No—where's she at? She too homely to come out in the daylight?"

I smiled. "She's probably asleep. She was up nearly all night, but I'm sure she'll be there when we bury Josh."

"I can't believe Josh had a wife somewhere all this time and never one time mentioned her," Johnnie said as he hammered in one last nail and then stepped back to inspect our work.

"Well, he did," I said, "but he never told me about her till the night you and him had that fight at Alamocitas."

"Do you think he ever planned on going back?"

"Said he couldn't—but yeah, I think he figured on goin' back someday."

It got quiet for a minute or so, and then I said, "Do you ever think about going home?"

Johnnie laughed and shook his head and then reached inside a pocket for his makin's.

"Yeah," Ab drawled in his slow Dixie way, "I think

123

about goin' home sometimes . . . someday I will, too."

I looked at Ab, so much younger than me or Johnnie, and I laughed. "Yeah . . . just like Josh did."

We rolled Josh up in a sheet and put him in the coffin. We put his boots and spurs in beside him and laid his hat on his chest, then we nailed the top down and got Lloyd Franks to help us carry him downstairs and across the draw to the cemetery while Mary Franks, Lloyd Franks's wife, and Lillie came out of the hotel and followed us.

It was cloudy, windy and shivering cold as we lowered Josh into the narrow grave and covered him up with dirt. I was sad that Josh had died, but I knew it must have been his time to go—that's the way a cowboy usually looks at such things, sort of like God threw a hoolihan loop from heaven that had Josh's name on it and was leadin' him home. That makes covering a friend's grave easier.

After we had the coffin covered, we all stood around in the cold looking down at the mound of earth. It didn't seem right, there not being a preacher there to say the words about Jesus and the cross and judgment and eternal life that are supposed to be said at a funeral, but none of us knew how to do it. Finally I took off my hat and, in a broad manner of speaking, starting singing: "In the sweet by and by . . ." Slowly, Ab and Johnnie and Lloyd Franks took off their hats too and started singing in the cold with me, the wind blowing their hair like it was mine: ". . . we will meet on that beautiful shore."

Mary Franks was solemn but didn't sing—mostly she just humped her back to the wind and looked cold.

Lillie didn't sing either, but she hung her head and cried while we did, and I thought that was sweet and nice, her only barely knowing Josh, but crying for him anyway. A man ought to have tears, preferably a woman's tears, fall into his fresh-dug grave dirt.

Yeah, I was glad that Lillie was there to put her tears on Josh's mound. And I was proud, too, especially as I saw Johnnie turn his head and look at Lillie from head to toe as she stood crying in the cold with bowed head. I was proud that Lillie was mine.

As soon as the service, such as it was, was over and we'd put our hats back on our heads and Lillie was walking toward the hotel with Mary and Lloyd Franks, I said to her, "Lillie?" She stopped and turned around. "Lillie, this is Ab Deacons and Johnnie Lester, friends of ours who are goin' to take our place at Trujillo Camp. Boys, this is Lillie Johnson."

"Ma'am," Johnnie and Ab both said, tipping their hats.

"Glad to meet you," Lillie said coldly, with only a faint smile, and then turned sharply around and walked toward the hotel.

"That 'her'?" Johnnie asked as we watched Lillie walking away. "The woman that's changin' your life? The one that's pretty and nice as that canyon you were talkin' about? The one that makes you want to put down roots and homestead? The one that makes you want to trade trail dust for crop dust?"

"That may be goin' a little too far"—I laughed—"but that's her."

"Or is she just a horsin' dry mare that you'd like to cut off from the herd and drive over the hill for an hour or so?"

I looked hard at Johnnie.

"Just what in the hell do you mean by that, Johnnie?" I asked.

Johnnie squinted an eye and seemed to think for a few seconds, and then he said, "Aw, hell . . . nothin', Casey. . . . Ab, whadaya say we get on out to Trujillo Camp?"

"I'll come with you," I said. "I need to take the company horses me an' Josh were ridin' to Trujillo Camp and get our horses. I'll get our beds and the little stuff we had outa the house."

"You can stay awhile, Casey," Ab said. "I don't give a goddamn what rule number three says."

"No . . . I'm kinda ready to get moved over to Rana Canyon and get that rock cabin fixed up."

"You really want to do that?" Johnnie asked.

"More than I've ever wanted anything else in my life," I said.

Before I left Endee I went upstairs to find Lillie. She was cleaning the room Josh had died in. She said she was tired and was going to try to sleep as soon as she had the room clean. She hardly looked at me.

I wanted to hold her, but I still hadn't bathed or shaved. "I'm going to get our things at Trujillo and take them to Rana Canyon," I said. "I'm going to start work on that cabin in the mornin', Lillie, but I'll be back here tomorrow night to see you. Maybe we won't be so tired by then. Lillie, I—"

"Casey! We're ready to go!" Johnnie yelled from outside.

"See you tomorrow night, Lillie," I said. "Lillie . . ."—I had my hat in my hand—"I'm fixin' that cabin up for us. After I get it at least tolerable . . . I'm going to ask you to be my wife."

Lillie had her back to me, but I saw her muscles tighten when I said that. But she didn't say she didn't want me to ask her. To me, the way I was thinking, that was the same as saying she loved me and wanted to be Mrs. Casey Wills forever and ever.

"Casey! We're leavin'!"

"See you tomorrow night, Lillie," I said as I backed out of the room.

We didn't talk much as we rode to Trujillo Camp. We had a lot on our minds and we were tired. I hadn't had any sleep in over two days.

The first thing we did when we got to Trujillo was for all three of us to put our ropes on old Plato and drag him out of the corral. After that, Johnnie gathered the horses out of the horse trap and penned them while Ab and I got my and Josh's beds and other stuff in the house ready to tie on a packsaddle.

In another hour I was standing in front of the saddle house with two of my and Josh's horses saddled and the other two loaded with our beds and what little other belongings we had.

"What're you gonna do with Josh's saddle and horses?" Johnnie asked.

"Me an' Josh had a little debt hangin' over our heads when he died." I told them about the happenings with Tatum Stagg and finished up by saying, "So I figure the money I got left put with Josh's horses ought to square us with the son of a bitch." I hadn't had time to think about Stagg much since Josh got hung to Plato, or the fact that he had stolen cattle right from under our noses, made us look like fools and gotten us fired. Ordinarily, I'd have gone on the warpath with him damn quick. God knows that I'd gone on the warpath before for a lot less. But there wasn't anything ordinary about my life anymore, especially not since Lillie had suddenly become part of it. She was practically all I thought about. She *was* all I thought about without extreme effort. But right then I exerted that sort of effort long enough to think about what Tatum Stagg had done, and, while I still didn't react like I normally would have, I said, "I think I'll whip his ass after I give his money back to him."

"We'd sure like to watch," Ab said.

"I'll invite you," I told them. "Just give me a couple of days."

There was something else I'd been thinking about since just after the funeral, and the reason I could think about it was because it involved Lillie. I thought I'd clear it up before I stepped on my gray. "Johnnie . . . what you said about maybe me just wantin' to cut Lillie outa the herd and drive her over the hill for an hour or so? Well, I don't feel about her that way. I mean to—"

"Maybe I wasn't talkin' so much about you, Casey," Johnnie said, "as I was her."

"Now just what in the hell do you mean, Johnnie?"

Johnnie bit his lip for a second and then said, "Well, Casey, I mean . . . maybe she wouldn't be so hard to cut out and take over the hill as a man would think. Maybe she's been taken over the hill before. Maybe she's been taken over a lot of hills and brought back and throwed in the herd lots of times before, Casey."

I hit Johnnie as hard as I could with my fist right in the corner of his mouth. I didn't hold nothing back.

"What 'n the hell are you doin', Casey!" Ab yelled.

As Johnnie was trying to get up he said, "She's Raven, Casey, the whore from Tascosa that—"

I didn't care if Johnnie was still down. I hit him

again. I tried to drive him into the ground like a railroad spike. Then I stood over him and said, "I'll kill you, Johnnie—goddamn you, I swear I'll kill you! You filthy-mouthed son of—"

Johnnie tackled me around my knees, and we went to the ground together.

"Goddammit!" Ab said. "Hell! Y'all just go ahead and kill each other. I'll be damned if I'm gonna wear myself out tryin' to keep either one of you alive!" Then he sat down on the doorstep of the saddle house and rolled a cigarette.

Before long me and Johnnie were both about out of vinegar. I still had plenty of heart, I just didn't have the muscle to go with it. I still wanted to get the right lick in on Johnnie's head so it would bust open like a September watermelon and scatter his brains in the corral so much a dozen chickens couldn't have scratched around and found all the chunks in a week. Barring that, I would have settled for getting my hands around his throat and choking him until his eyeballs popped and his tongue lolled out on the ground. But my arms were too heavy to bring about the mayhem and destruction my heart desired, and my lungs couldn't suck in enough cold air to keep me alive unless I leaned over and grabbed my knees.

I guess Johnnie was in no better fighting shape than I was, but instead of holding his knees, he was holding the fence and hanging his head down between his arms.

Ab was still sitting in the saddle house door with his legs crossed rolling another cigarette and breathing as easy as you please. I couldn't help but think of the time not long ago when all four of us were peeing off a rimrock and Josh had said to Johnnie, "You oughta learn to be more like Ab. You see how he can stand here and pee and mind his own business."

I finally got enough air in my lungs so I could straighten up, and when I did I staggered over to the horses and climbed up on the gray. I gathered up the reins of the other horses and started for the gate.

"You think I wanted to tell you, Casey?" Johnnie said.

I stopped just inside the gate. "You're wrong," I said.

"I ain't sayin' you shouldn't marry her if that's what you've got your mind made up to do. I just thought you ought to know the truth before you did. Now you know. . . . So you go ahead and do as you damn well please."

"Lillie's a widowed lady from New York!" I said.

"She may be," Johnnie said, still trying to get his breath, "but she's Raven from Tascosa, too."

"But she's been here over a year," I insisted, "and you—"

"Okay," Johnnie said on another long breath, "I lied about trading her the wolf ears and being with her when we all went to town after the wagon pulled in. I didn't see her at all then, but I wanted to make you think I did. I was up there in that room alone, and I just took off my clothes and stood in front of the window to fool you."

I started out the gate again, figuring my case was proven and Johnnie would have apologized if he hadn't been so hardheaded. "But," he said, and I stopped again, "she *was* there when I was in Tascosa a year or so before. I didn't . . . have her, but I promised myself that the next time I was in town I would, and she's the one I thought about every night the last two months of the works. I knew who she was the instant I saw her when we were burying Josh. I didn't even have to think about it. I wish it wasn't true."

I looked at Johnnie a few seconds, hating him, and then I looked over at Ab. "See ya, Ab," I said as I trotted out the gate.

CHAPTER
16

My plans, before the set-to with Johnnie that is, had been to get my and Josh's horses and gear from Trujillo Camp and go straight to Rana Canyon and the little rock cabin beside the Blue Hole. Once there, I would build a fire inside that little cabin and sleep beside it until daylight. At that time it had been two and a half days since I'd had any sleep, and my body and brain were constantly reminding me of that fact. But, even as tired as I was, I didn't leave Trujillo Camp on a northwesterly course at all. Instead, I rode south again, leading the three horses behind me as a cold sun set before me. I *had* to go back to Endee— not the next day after I woke up, but right then, before I ever even lay down to sleep.

It was a couple of hours past dark when I rode up to the hotel—the hotel that was Endee—again. The lanterns had been lit downstairs and, as I tied the horses to the railing outside, I heard laughter inside.

I opened the door, and the laughter faded away.

Stagg's men—Eddie, Matt and Nate—were standing at the bar along the north end of the room. Lloyd Franks was behind the bar pouring drinks for them. Franks and the three men looked at me and I looked at them. Then I looked at the two people sitting at a table with a bottle of whiskey between them. A man and a woman . . . Lillie and Tatum Stagg.

"Hello, Wills," Stagg said. Then he pushed a chair back with a foot and said, "Sit down and I'll buy you a drink."

I walked across the floor and stopped at the table. I looked at Lillie and she looked down. My heart was beating fast.

"Sit down," Stagg said again.

"I came to settle some accounts," I said as I started pulling off my gloves. I couldn't seem to take my eyes off Lillie's face. She glanced up at me once and then looked down toward the floor again. She hadn't looked me in the eye yet.

"How much did Josh owe you, Mr. Franks?" I asked.

"Nothin'," Franks said.

Now I looked at him, and he read the question in my eyes, so he said again—"Your partner didn't owe anything, Mr. Wills."

"The whiskey," I said. "I know he drank at least two bottles."

"Mr. Stagg there . . . uh, he paid for the whiskey," Franks said.

I looked at Stagg, and he smiled and shrugged his shoulders.

"The room he was in," I said, looking back up at Franks and pulling off my second glove. "Room two twelve. Two days and two nights. How much?"

Franks fidgeted with a rag he was holding.

"How much?" I said again, taking my eyes off Lillie and looking at Franks.

"Well . . . that's Lillie's room, and it's already been paid for—in advance," Franks answered.

My eyes fell to Lillie again. She dropped her head and put it in her hands. *"Your room,* Lillie?" I asked softly.

But Lillie didn't answer the question. So, with my eyes still on her, I said, "Who pays the rent on two twelve, Mr. Franks? . . . On Lillie's room . . . On the room where Josh died?"

Franks didn't answer.

"Casey . . . please," Lillie said in a weak voice, barely lifting her head.

"Who?" I said loudly.

Franks hesitated a few seconds and then said, "Mr. Stagg there pays the rent on that room a month at a time, like I said—in advance."

"Mr. Franks," I said. "Does he *stay* in that room sometimes?"

"Casey. . . . Please don't!" Lillie sobbed. She sobbed, and the men standing at the bar snickered.

Stagg poured himself another drink and said in a go-to-hell voice, "I pay the goddamn rent, don't I?"

"But . . . Lillie," I said—no, I didn't just *say* the words, I *breathed* those words, and they were full of the pain that I felt, a pain deeper and more terrible than any pain I had ever known—"what about . . . what about . . . What about *us,* Lillie?"

The men at the bar laughed again, and louder this time, much louder. Tatum Stagg laughed, too. Even Lloyd Franks laughed. Everybody in Endee laughed as Lillie flew across the room and ran up the stairs.

I don't know how long the men laughed, but as they did so, and as I stood frozen beside Stagg's table with my gloves in my hand and my heavy coat still buttoned, the truth about Lillie, about Josh's death and even about the timing of Stagg stealing the XIT cattle came as clear and as cold—and as merciless— to me as a cloudless, high plains, midwinter's night. Numbed by that merciless truth, I reeled and staggered outside and closed the door to the wild laughter inside.

I slowly untied the horses and mounted my gray, trying to sort things out in my mind as I rode north across the draw. The hurt inside me was deep, and I don't think it could have been any more complete than it was. I felt gutted, hollowed out like the carcass of some old cow who has lain out in the heat and the cold and the wind and the sun so long she's nothing more than stiff rawhide and chalky bones. An old cow like that is really not a cow anymore, she's just a shell where a cow used to be. That's how I felt—like a shell where a man used to be.

It was a dark night that night. The moon in the east was behind some clouds, and the ten thousand stars in the part of the sky not clouded over gave off hardly any light at all. In fact, it seemed like the stars were farther away and colder than they had ever been since eternity began. The gray was more or less wandering on his own, as a shell of a man is hardly capable of setting a direction, even of setting a direction on a saddle horse, and in a few minutes he, the gray, came against the sagging fence around Endee's cemetery and stopped.

I looked at the fresh pile of dirt on the other side of the fence in the dim, cold light of night. The thought of Josh lying dead in his grave was now much more painful than it had been a few hours ago—when I thought God had thrown a long-loop hoolihan and led Josh out of earth's remuda of men to a good country of forever green grass and clear waters. Now I knew differently. God's rope had never left His righteous hand. It was Tatum Stagg's long rope of dishonor that Josh—and myself—had gotten rimfired by. Stagg, with the help of Lillie's white lies, had brought about our downfall on the XIT and caused Josh's death. Even though the picture made me wince in pain, I could see Lillie—no, not Lillie but Raven—inviting Josh up to her room—to Stagg's room—to have a drink with her. And of course the promises of other pleasures spoken with those dark eyes—my God! The same unspoken promises I had seen but dismissed at Trujillo Camp as the foolish wanderings of an indecent cowboy mind! One drink. And then another. More promises of other pleasures, maybe by now not so silent and subtle. Now another drink, a bigger one. And two more. And . . .

I wrapped the lead ropes of the other horses around the saddle horn and pulled my makin's out of a coat pocket. I separated one cigarette paper from the rest, troughed it and poured some Durham into it. Then I pulled the string shut on the tobacco sack with my teeth and put the sack back into my pocket. I sat there a few seconds looking at the paper with the tobacco in it and thinking. I rolled the paper between my thumb and fingers, but before I licked it with my tongue I pointed it toward Josh's grave and said, "I told you not to ride old Plato that mornin'. . . . She just kept pourin' the whiskey down you, didn't she? And you never were one to say whoa to whiskey—even when *you* were buyin' it. But it was killin' you this time, Josh, and you just kept adrinkin'. . . . And then when you passed out and got sick, or whichever came first, Tatum sent Lillie out to Trujillo Camp to entertain *me*."

I licked the cigarette and stuck it between my lips, struck a match on the top button of my Levi's, lit the cigarette and drew smoke deep into my lungs. Then I laughed a little bit, not outside where anybody could've told I was laughing even if there had've been anyone there except me and the horses and the ghosts of Endee. But it was enough to convince me I wasn't as hollowed out as I felt. I had to laugh when I imagined Lillie telling Stagg about being at Trujillo Camp with me: "That cowboy Casey Wills? He's the most easily entertained man I've ever spent the night with." And then I could see Lillie and Stagg laughing at me as they passed the bottle back and forth and walked upstairs to room 212.

When I opened Endee's door again some thirty minutes after reeling out under the blow and the weight of the truth about me and Lillie and Josh and Tatum Stagg, the three men were still at the bar and Lloyd Franks was still behind the bar pouring drinks for them, but Stagg was not in sight. It wasn't hard to figure where he was, though, and when I opened the door to room 212, with Stagg's men close behind me, I found out I was right in my figuring.

Stagg was lying on the bed, and Lillie was standing in front of the window.

"What in the hell?" Stagg said, swinging his feet off the side of the bed and standing up.

"Casey!" Lillie said as she turned and saw me

standing in the doorway. She was crying, and she came toward me. "I didn't know it would happen like this, Casey. I didn't know. I'm sorry. Please—"

Then Stagg came between us, shoved her back with one arm and said, "What're you doin' up here, Wills?"

By then Eddie, Matt and Nate were standing behind me. Lillie had moved again to the window with her back to me.

"Well, Wills?" Stagg said, his voice getting louder. "What in the hell do you want? More money?" Then he laughed again. "That's it, ain't it, Wills? You think I oughta give you some more money, don't you?" He pulled out his wallet. "How much were you figuring on? Another fifty maybe? Seventy-five? Hell, we didn't get but thirty-three head. That damn storm had 'em all scattered and bushed up. Well, come on, damn it, and name your price. Here's a hundred! Don't say I ain't tryin' to be fair."

I looked at Lillie standing in front of the window and then I looked at Stagg and the hundred-dollar bill at the end of his outreached hand.

Then I dropped a hand inside my coat pocket and pulled out a wad of money in bills and coins and dropped it all at Stagg's feet, all except for five dollars and two cents that I kept in my hand. "Keep your money, Stagg," I said. "And here's the money you thought would buy me and Josh. But, like I told you the night you came to see us, you were at the wrong camp. Well, I'm tellin' you again, Stagg, you came to the wrong camp that night. Me and Josh never intended to keep that money or the money you left tied to a fence post later, we were just too busy earnin' a honest living to get it back to you before now, but there it is.

"It's all there too, except for forty dollars and two cents. I'll leave Josh's horses tied up outside for you. I figure they're worth thirty-five dollars. That leaves five dollars and two cents, and I've got it right here in my hand, but I'm not giving it to you." I walked past Stagg and stopped right behind Lillie. "Here's the two cents you loaned me to mail that letter with— Raven," I said. "And here's five dollars . . . for the time you spent with me at Trujillo Camp and Rana Canyon."

Lillie turned around and looked at me with red eyes. Hurting eyes. Disbelieving eyes. Her cheeks were wet with tears.

I reached past Lillie and laid the money on the windowsill. I couldn't look into her eyes any longer.

"I'll be coming to get those thirty-three head of cows and whatever calves they had on them," I said, "the ones you took from the XIT Trujillo Camp country while me and Josh were at Trujillo Camp. It'll be easier if you'll just send your men here back with them in the mornin'."

The laughter came again from Stagg and his men.

"Hell," Stagg said, "I've stole ten times that many goddamn cows from the XIT before you ever showed up, and I'll steal ten times that many after you're gone!"

"I guess that's between you and them," I said. "The thirty-three head you stole three days ago is between you and me."

"What's this," he said, "some kind of goddamn cowboy pride or something?"

"Yeah," I said, "that's what it is."

Stagg laughed. "Haven't you heard about what the Bible says about pride going before a fall?"

"I've heard it," I told him, "but I never really understood it. I figure we're all going to fall sooner or later. The question is, do we fall with pride or without?"

"You're a crazy son of a bitch," Stagg said.

I buttoned my coat and said, "And don't you ever forget it." And then I turned and walked down the hall.

Behind me I heard Stagg say, "Give him a quick lesson and send him on his way, boys. And give his goddamn money back to him—he earned it."

Then Stagg's men were on me, and the last thing I remember hearing was Lillie shouting, *"No, Tatum! No!"*

CHAPTER
17

Luck was on my side during the scuffle with Stagg's men that night when they rained down on me in the hallway of the hotel at Endee. No, I didn't whip the three or even come close to it—the luck I had was that one of the earliest blows the Stagg boys were so generously bestowing upon my skull knocked me out and I didn't have to witness the remainder of the bloody fracas.

It was a strange night all the way around, and it didn't end when the hall lights went out, but from then on fact and fiction became entangled and it was hard to tell which was which. Looking back upon the night by the light of the next day, however, I did conclude that the part about a spider who could spin a web across the mouth of a canyon, large and strong enough to catch and hold a horse and rider, was probably not true.

The first time I saw the spider he was up high on the rim of a narrow canyon, where he was looking down upon his web. The web was vibrating furiously because Josh and Plato had ridden into it. Plato was spinning like a top trying to get out, but all he was doing was getting him and Josh wrapped up tighter and tighter. I was frantically coming down the canyon on the little dun XIT horse with the hole in his ear to get to them, cussing Plato under my breath for being such a stupid son of a bitch. When the spider saw me coming to help Josh, he started down from the canyon's rim.

The next thing I know, there is a woman standing in front of me in the middle of the narrow canyon. I pull the dun to a sliding stop a few feet in front of her. I look at her bare feet and work my way up with my eyes. I see, all covered by a thin, black, wispy gown, a wonderful pair of satinlike legs, the swell of hips and then of breasts. I gasp and the dun snorts because we have heard something that sounds like the hiss of a giant snake. I jerk my head up and see what is making the noise—a spider the size of a man's fist sitting on the woman's shoulder. Then I look at the woman's face. It is hard, twisted, contorted—frightening. But I recognize her. It is Lillie!

Lillie speaks—"I love you, Casey"—but her voice is not the sweet and gentle voice I had known before. Now it is a deep, raspy voice. "Yes, I love you, Casey," the spider on her shoulder mocks in a voice like only a black spider could have—high-pitched, crude and cold. "Don't you want to come closer? Don't you want to come closer?"

"No!" Lillie rasps. "Don't come any closer, Casey. Not as long as *it's* alive. . . . Shoot it, Casey! Kill it!"

"You can't!" The spider roars in laughter that

shakes the canyon walls. "You can't kill me without killing her. *Ha! Ha!*"

"Kill it!" Lillie screams.

"Lillie," I say.

"Raven!" screeches the spider.

"Casey, please!" screams Lillie. "It's *not* my soul!" The spider is now growing in front of my eyes. Now it's suddenly as big as Lillie's head.

"Where's Josh?" I demand.

"Where's Josh? Where's Josh?" mocks the spider. "Don't you want to come to bed with me? Don't you want to come to bed with me?"

"No!" Lillie screams and starts struggling with the spider, trying to push it off her shoulder.

"You'll die!" the spider hisses. "You can't live without me!"

But suddenly Lillie *does* push him off. As she starts falling toward the ground, I see her face become beautiful again. But the spider is coming back for her! I jerk my rope down, shake out a quick loop and throw a fast and hard hoolihan that catches him around the middle. Now he's coming up my rope! The dun boogers and starts pitching . . .

And that's the way that dream ended.

Then, after what seemed like an eternity passed, I felt like I was in a place of sweet stillness. A place of comforting warmth and peacefulness. A place of comfort and sweetness and peacefulness that can only be described by one word—home. Soft, sweet-smelling hair caressed my face, and warm and tender lips brushed the corner of my mouth.

Then I woke up. After a few seconds of blinking my eyes, rubbing the sore spots on my head and looking around in a daze, I realized I was lying on my bedroll and my bedroll was on the ground in the little rock cabin in Rana Canyon beside the Blue Hole. Not only that, but there were a few coals beside me where a fire had been and sitting just at the edge of those graying coals was my coffeepot.

Something else—on the ground beside the coffee-pot, underneath a rock, was a five-dollar bill.

I picked the money up and looked at it, trying to figure out where it had come from, and then stuck it in my coat pocket. In the other coat pocket I found the money I had tried to give back to Stagg the night before.

I felt the pot. It wasn't hot, but it was warm and so was the coffee inside. I filled the cup sitting beside the pot and sipped the coffee slowly, trying to remember what all had happened the night before, and trying to remember riding all the way to Rana Canyon after the Stagg boys were finished with my lesson. But that lesson—the beginning of it and not the ending—was as far as my memory of the night went.

I remembered the stupid dream I'd had about Lillie and the spider and shook my head and smiled when I thought about it. But when I remembered the comfort and peacefulness I'd dreamed about, I only felt comfortable and peaceful again. I also remembered the feeling of warmth and dropped my eyes to the graying coals again.

I stood up and stretched and felt the soreness of my body. Then I walked to the door of the cabin and saw my horses hobbled and grazing outside and my saddle lying on top of my saddle blankets beside the cabin. If I'd done all of this for myself, I sure couldn't remember a bit of it. Then I saw a couple of footprints in the dust of the doorway, and I knelt down to study them closer.

There was no doubt about it, the footprints in the dust I was studying were not mine—they were much too small. Then in the rotting wood of the doorframe I saw something else and carefully pulled it out and stretched it between my hands and looked at it a long time—a black hair a foot and a half long. I remembered the part of the dream—one of the best parts—when I felt soft, sweet-smelling hair caressing my face and soft, warm lips brushing the corners of my mouth.

The five dollars. The small footprints. The long black hair. Suddenly I knew . . . I knew Lillie had been there! She had brought me there!

What I didn't know was why.

The gray and I came out of Rana Canyon alone. We traveled west for fifteen, maybe twenty, miles until we came to a rocky rim overlooking Revuelto Creek. Tatum Stagg had told me and Josh that he had a place west of Endee, so it wasn't hard to figure that somewhere along the Revuelto a man should find it. But north, toward the Canadian River and rougher country, or south, toward flatter country? I decided south, the direction I would have chosen for a ranch if I'd been stealing cattle from the XIT and not really caring to hide them, for XIT cattle came from Texas and this was New Mexico, a place where the XIT was as loved as smallpox. A place where Texas law meant nothing. And from here even the nearest New Mexico law was in Las Vegas, a hundred and fifty miles away. Yes, south . . . to a place among big cottonwoods where the creek widened out and the flatter country met the breaks.

It was just such a spot as that where I found the Stagg Ranch, on the east side of the creek at the foot of a small mesa, among a growth of cottonwoods. From where I watched, among some hilltop cedars on the west side of the creek, I could see the ranch was a ramshackle sort of place, with the house, bunkhouse, barns and corrals thrown together to begin with and then patched and repatched. There were no guards, but there were three men in the corrals, and I could hear cattle bawling and even smell branding smoke on the still, cold air of December.

I didn't spend time drawing up a very fancy plan. Most fancy plans go to hell in the first few minutes anyway. I just rode the gray down from my hilltop, across the creek and up to the fence of the corral.

The men were talking and laughing until I rode up. Then they just stood and looked at me. They were Stagg's three men. Stagg himself was not in sight. They looked at me like I was crazy to just ride in like I had.

"Mornin', fellers," I said as I looked at the cows in the corral and counted them. Thirty-three head, most still wearing a plain XIT on the right rib cage, but a few—six or seven—with the brand already changed to Stagg's Butterfly Ax.

"This all the cattle y'all could steal the other night, huh? That ain't many, even in a snowstorm. Hell, me and Josh have run off more than this by accident. But then I could tell by lookin' at you nesters that you'd be hard-pressed to gather a decent settin' of eggs. Well hell, boys, open up this gate and run 'em out and I'll take 'em back home."

The men looked at one another like they couldn't believe what they were hearing, and then they laughed. Eddie, the tall, muscular one with a dark complexion and a drooping mustache, said, "Are you damn drunk or just damn crazy, Wills?"

I pulled out my makin's and spooled a smoke while they watched and glanced at one another and grinned. After I'd lit the cigarette I thumbed the match away and said, "Well, I ain't drunk, 'cause I've been drunk before and I know what it feels like, and it don't feel like I feel right now. I could be crazy, though," I said and winked. "I punched cows with a crazy man one time in Arizona around Prescott who cut the throats of three gringos and a Mexican one night when he got up to pee, and then he just crawled back in his bedroll and went to sleep. He didn't give a damn about nothin'. That's what makes me think I could be crazy too—I just don't give a damn. Now let's get this gate open."

They started forward.

"Of course, I ain't so crazy I'd just ride in here alone without havin' a couple of fellers up there in the rocks with rifles just dyin' to shoot something. Uh-huh! I wouldn't look up there if I was you, not any more than just a quick sidewards glance, 'cause them fellers *are* crazy. They got a bet on which one of *them* can shoot one of *you* in the eye from up there first—I think it's the left eye they're bettin' on. But hell! I don't know if they can shoot as good as they claim they can or not. All I know is that when I take my hat off and scratch my head like this"—I took my hat off and scratched my head—"they're supposed to cock their rifles and balance your heads on top of the front sights. And"—I held my hat in my hand and looked at it—"when I put my hat back on they're supposed to shoot, unless, of course, you boys start shootin' before

147

I get a chance to put it on." I knocked dust off of my hat with my other hand. "I mean, you could shoot me out of my saddle right now, but just because I never got a chance to put my hat on don't mean the war's already over and the troops have gone home to their brides."

"You're a crazy goddamn lunatical son of a bitch," Eddie said, "if you think we're gonna believe there's someone up in those rocks." That's what he said, but, just in case he was wrong, I noticed none of them were looking directly at the rocks on top of the mesa. The way it looked to me right then was that they had called my hand, but, by not coming after me, they hadn't raised. Since my hole card was about equal to the deuce of nothing, I had some aversion to showing it.

So I raised. And how I raised was stupid and dangerous. But I wasn't lying when I said I didn't give a damn. A man gets in that frame of mind sometimes, and when he does it seems he wants to see how far he can go, how far he can push the edge back or how close to the edge he can get without falling off. It's the same sort of feeling a cowboy gets now and then when he steps in the middle of a horse that's tight as a fiddle string and tiptoeing around like a ballerina. He knows he can probably ease that horse around until he's warmed up and the hump is out of his back. He also knows he can crowd that same horse a little and turn him instantly into a four-legged, squalling, blind-pitching cyclone. Nearly every time the cowboy will choose the former course—the safer course—of action. But every now and then, when he's in the right frame of mind and not giving a damn about anything, he'll just step in the saddle and bog his spurs in that waiting cyclone's shoulders just to see what will happen. I guess a man has to be crazy like that sometimes to make being sane the rest of the time tolerable.

I changed hands with my hat and lifted my old Colt out of its holster. I ran my tongue out of my mouth as far as it would go, rolled my eyes around in their sockets and raised the Colt, putting the muzzle against my right temple and cocking the hammer. "Crazy as a loon," I said, mocking Eddie. Then I lowered the hammer on the Colt and tossed it to him. "Be careful, it's loaded," I said.

Eddie caught the Colt instinctively.

"Now," I said, "let's see *you* point it at my head and cock the hammer. Well, go on—if I'm so crazy you ought to just go ahead and blast and put me out of my misery."

He was obviously bewildered, but he also obviously did *not* lift the Colt and point it at me. I winked at him and said, "Smart move." Then I rode up to him, and he handed my Colt back to me—butt first and very carefully!

"Okay," I said. "Now you boys hand me your guns and unsaddle your horses and turn 'em loose. Then I'd be obliged to you if you'd open the gate and turn this little old handful of cows out into the great yonder."

After the last cow had trotted out the gate I said, "Well, boys, I can't say how much fun this has been, but I guess it's hasta luego and happy trails time for now. Tell Stagg I said it was a shame that I missed him. Good-bye now."

149

CHAPTER
18

Tatum Stagg's ranch on the Revuelto Creek was a little over twenty miles from the XIT fence and almost due west of Trujillo Camp. The country was flat to rolling, covered with grass and sagebrush and easy traveling for a small herd of cows ready to get back to their home range. The cows were either longhorn or some sort of longhorn cross and made for traveling. There was a dun-colored longhorn cow with a tight bag in the bunch who had left a calf somewhere back in Texas, and she was anxious to get home and find it. She took the lead as soon as we left the Revuelto Creek breaks country. She dropped her horned head a little, hit a long-strided walk and seldom looked back or to either side, only straight ahead, toward Texas and the XIT. All I had to do was to keep the drags caught up with her. She was better than having Josh along. She really wasn't, of course, but that's what I would have told Josh if I'd had the chance.

I don't know much about the hereafter. Still, it was

nice to ride along behind those cows thinking about Josh watching from *somewhere,* laughing as I bluffed Stagg's men into letting me have the cattle and now feeling as satisfied as I was that the black mark against our cowboy record would be erased in a few more hours.

It wouldn't mean anything to anyone—but me and Josh—that the few head of cattle Stagg stole from the Trujillo Camp country of the XIT while we were living at the camp would be returned. Stagg had stolen a lot more cattle from the outfit than the thirty-three while we were there, and others had stolen more than that at other times and places along that western boundary. The XIT lost more head of cattle than that each week to wolves, more than that each week to bogs and blackleg. In wet summers they lost many more than that each week to screwworms alone. No, that particular thirty-three head wasn't going to make or break an outfit that owned over a hundred thousand head. The bigwigs in Chicago didn't know they had been stolen four days ago, and they would never know I had returned them.

But to me it was a matter of principle. If Josh was sitting up in heaven amid beauty and luxury, or if he was lying forever dead and unknowing underneath six feet of cold dirt, the memory of who and what he had been was still inside *me,* and it was *that,* along with the pride I had in myself, that demanded those thirty-three head be returned. I'd heard it said one time, in a vine-covered church along the Little Kanawha River in West Virginia, that pride is one of the greatest of sins, but, like I'd told Stagg, I'd never been able to figure that one out. You take away a cowboy's pride and you take away about all he has.

In some kinds of country four or five miles can be a long ways, but in a prairie country where one wide, sage-covered draw looks like all the rest and where you can look in the distance and see nothing but more distance and where the horizon lays way out there somewhere past forever, four or five miles seems like nothing. Even when you're making good time with thirty-three head of cows and you cover four or five miles in one hour, it seems like you're treading water in a big ocean. And when you keep looking back over your shoulder toward the western horizon that lies past forever in the distance, expecting at any time to see tiny black dots on it that could just as well be sharks on that ocean it feels like you are treading water in, you want to whip those cows on the butt and you cuss them for moving so slow. But you know you are going as fast as you can with them if you expect to get all of them to Texas—to the shore.

But the sharks were coming. I first saw them as the tiny black specks I had been looking for. But they didn't appear on the western horizon. They appeared in the south, in the direction of Endee, riding to cut me off from Texas. I knew they would come, of course. I might have been crazy, but I wasn't stupid. I just hoped I could beat them to the XIT fence and run the cows back onto the XIT. Beyond that, just like I'd told Stagg's men at the ranch, I didn't give a damn.

I kicked the cows into a run, taking my catch rope down and whooping and hollering and dragging long-horn hair off high-tailed butts. There wasn't any use to conserve energy now.

I topped a small rise, and way out there in front oɪ me for the first time I could make out the outline oɪ the house and barn at Trujillo Camp and I could see the windmill there too, no more than three miles away. I *had* made good time with the cows. It had been about five hours since I'd left Stagg's place, and I was already almost to Texas.

Almost.

I looked at the black dots coming at me from the south. They weren't as tiny now as they had been just a couple of minutes ago even. And if you looked close enough, they weren't just black dots against the caprock anymore. Now those black dots were men on horseback, riding in a long lope, angling toward a spot somewhere between my herd and Texas.

By the time I'd gone another half mile east, the riders angling up from the south had gone a mile north and were between me and Texas.

I let the cows slow down to a walk again and thought about running. But instead of running, I stopped the gray and rolled a cigarette. By the time I got the cigarette lit, Stagg and his men had stopped the cows and turned them back. And it wasn't just Stagg and his men—Lillie was with them, riding a short, rangy-looking bay. She avoided my eyes.

The first thing Stagg said when they rode up to me was "Goddamn you, Wills."

"Well, goddamn you too, Stagg," I said. Then I looked at Lillie and added, "Goddamn us all."

"He's crazy!" Nate declared. "Pretty soon he'll loll his tongue and—"

"*He's* crazy, Nate?" Stagg said. "Where's the men he had with him?" Then Stagg looked at me again and said, "What in the hell do you think you're doing?"

"You know what I'm doin', Stagg," I said.

"Yeah, I know—you're pushin'. How much do you want? Five hundred? Six?"

"It's not about money, Stagg, it's—"

"Sure it is!" he said. *"Everything's* about money, Wills. Some people are just too embarrassed to admit it. Not me. I'm not trying to hide what I'm doing behind some phony principle. I steal for the money. And not Lillie either—she don't stay with me because I'm handsome and charming as hell or treat her like a queen and make her little old heart turn somersaults ever' time I touch her. She's mine because of the money I pay her. Me and Lillie are what we are, but at least we're up front about it. Why don't you try being the same? Now, how much money do you want? How much to get you out of the country? A thousand? I've got it at the ranch. We can all ride back there and—"

I looked Tatum Stagg in the eye. "You can take your thousand dollars and buy your way into hell with it," I told him. Then I glanced at Lillie and said, "Some people and some things aren't for sale."

"Oh goddamn!" Stagg said, laughing. "There's nothing funnier or more pathetic than a self-righteous cowboy who thinks being honest and broke is good. Do you think not taking my money means you're better than me?"

I nodded my head slowly and grinned. "You figure it out, Stagg."

"Get off your goddamn horse!" he ordered. When I didn't do it, he said, "Nate!" and Nate drew his revolver out of his holster and cocked it.

I got off my horse, and Stagg got off his. We stood there facing each other, and then he unbuckled his gun belt and tossed it aside. I unbuckled mine and tossed it aside too. Stagg said, "If you can get on your horse and ride off before I can get on mine, then I'll let you take the cows. If I get on mine first, me and the boys take the cows back to my ranch and you leave the country. Is it a deal?"

"Yeah," I told him. "It's a deal."

The other men all got off their horses and gathered around us as we shadowboxed each other. Then I saw an opening and hit Stagg on the nose with a quick right jab, but he was fast and while I was hitting him on the nose he hit me in the mouth, knocked out a bottom tooth, cut my lip and staggered me backwards.

I was addled and still rocking backwards when Stagg was in my face again. He hit me twice more, and I could feel the blood running down my cheek and taste it in my mouth. He was grinning then, and his men were cheering him on.

But I think I had more strength and less quit than he thought I did. When he came in to finish me off, I hit him in the pit of his stomach with all I could muster. That surprised him and took his air away for a second, which gave me a chance to hit his slack jaw with an upper cut that slammed his teeth together and snapped his head back. When his head came down, I put both hands together and, like chopping with an ax, hit him just underneath his left ear.

As I drew back to hit him again, thinking that blow might drive him into the ground, something was holding my arm back. That "something" of course was one of Stagg's men. And suddenly there was a man holding each arm.

As I struggled with the men holding me, Stagg came at me. "I said whoever can ride away, remember, Wills?" he growled as he kneed me in the groin. Then he hit me in the face. Again. Twice more. I lost count. Now there was no pain, just a numb, sinking feeling.

Then there was a loud shot, and I heard Lillie's voice scream, *"Stop it!"*

The world was spinning, and what I heard and saw I seemed to be hearing and seeing in a dream.

"Let him go!" Lillie screamed again. She had a rifle in her hands, pointed at all of us. She must have slipped it out of a scabbard while Stagg and I were fighting.

"I said to let him go!" Lillie again.

They did let me go, but I took one wobbly step away from them and sank to the ground. My knees just wouldn't hold me up.

"Lillie!" That was Stagg's voice. "Put that goddamn rifle down! Have you lost your mind?"

"Casey . . ." Lillie's voice was shaking and scared. "Get up, Casey."

"Lillie!" Stagg again.

"Shut up!" Lillie screamed. "Casey?" But I couldn't get up. I couldn't even talk. I could form some words in my head, but I couldn't get them to my mouth.

"I'm warning you, Lillie," Stagg said, not loud now but low and mean. "Drop that goddamn rifle or you'll be sorry. . . . Nate, toss me a gun."

"No! Don't, Tatum!" Lillie said, but I heard a hammer click back nonetheless.

"Now what're you going to do?" I heard Stagg ask. I managed to turn my head so I could see him. He had a cocked Colt held out at arm's length, aiming it at Lillie. I tried to tell Lillie to put the rifle down, but still the words would only form in my head and not on my lips.

"Casey . . . please." Lillie's voice, unsteady, unsure, confused, pleading. I gathered all my strength and tried to pull myself up, got to my knees and was trying to stand, wanting to help Lillie. I was afraid for her. I knew what she had gotten herself into, the corner she had backed herself into.

I looked at Stagg and saw the smile across his face, his fingers drawing tight around the butt of the Colt.

A word finally burst out of my mouth. One word. *"Lillie!"*

And then the roar of Stagg's gun.

Lillie wasn't shot out of the saddle, wasn't shot at all, as I was afraid she had been the instant the gun went off. But the little bay fell instantly out from underneath her, sending her sprawling on the ground in fear and shock, the rifle landing three feet from her. Stagg had killed the little bay with a bullet between the eyes, and now he was standing there laughing. "Now, Nate," he said with a satisfied air, "get that goddamn rifle."

Nate handed the rifle to Stagg and asked the inevitable question—"What're we gonna do with them?"

Stagg got on his horse. "Put her up here in the saddle in front of me."

Nate and one of the other men lifted Lillie off the ground, carried her over to Stagg's horse and put her in the saddle in front of Stagg.

"Now what about him?" Nate asked.

Stagg hesitated a second and then said, "Get his rope and put the loop around his feet."

I tried to stand again. Stagg rode close to me and kicked me hard in the ribs with the sharp toe of his boot. I went down again in pain, trying to catch my breath, unable to kick even as Nate slipped the small loop in my rope around my feet and pulled it snug.

"Now put the horn loop over his saddle horn," Stagg said. I was jolted with a sudden rush of panic but unable to fight back.

"Tie his bridle reins around the gray's neck so he won't be stepping on them," Stagg said. "Now then . . . Wills, you were in an awful mighty hurry to get back to the famous XIT, so I'm just gonna let you go there—without any cattle, of course. Your gray's used to bein' fed at the barn at Trujillo Camp, so I figure he ought to take you all the way there in a long lope. . . . Turn him loose and whip his ass, Nate."

"You sure, Tatum?" Nate asked.

"Yeah, goddammit, Nate, I'm sure," Stagg said. "Wills is about to the end of his rope." Then he quickly took his own rope and shook out two or three coils of it, moving toward the gray as he did so. With a laugh he said, "Say hello to the devil for me, Casey!" Then he whipped the gray's butt with his rope.

"No, Tatum, please!" screamed Lillie.

In a second all the slack was out of my rope, and I was snatched forward with a hard jerk, my arms and head flailing around uncontrollably as I was dragged across clumps of grass, sagebrush, bear grass, and prickly pear.

"Whoa!" I yelled to the gray. *"Whoa! Whoa! Whoa! . . .* Whoa . . . whoa." I tried feebly to get the knife in my right front britches pocket, but I couldn't manage it, I was bouncing too high.

"Ca . . . sey!" I heard Lillie scream from what seemed like a far and distant place—a place that I had been to one time but would never be allowed to return to again. I knew I was going to die by the way cowboys fear most—dragging to death at the end of a thirty-foot-catch rope, with my arms trailing helplessly over my head. One second I would be dragging on my stomach, and then I would hit something that would flip me over onto my back. Front and back. Back and front. Uncontrollable motion. Coat and shirt peeling off. Skin burning. "Whoa . . . wh-oa . . . wh-oa . . . wh-oa . . ." And then miraculously I was back home in West Virginia fishing from the bank of the Little Kanawha River and Momma was calling me to supper.

CHAPTER
19

For a while I didn't know if the gray had really drug me to hell or if it just felt like he had. But if he did, either he drug me all the way *through* hell and out the other side or else Johnnie Lester and Ab Deacons were in hell, too, because every time I opened my eyes and looked around I saw one, or both, of them.

Johnnie and Ab both swore the first thing I said was "Is Josh down here, too?" I expect they weren't telling the truth, but I never did know for sure.

For a while, I think before I even said anything or before Johnnie or Ab even knew that I wasn't still unconscious, I had trouble trying to remember what had happened and then I had trouble trying to decide if what I was remembering really *had* happened.

Three things I decided for sure—I was lying in a bedroll in the house at Trujillo Camp, it was dark outside and Johnnie and Ab were there. I could tell by the bacon grease and bandages on me that Johnnie and Ab had been nursing me, and as sore and peeled up as I was, what I remembered about being drug must have been true.

"How bad am I hurt?" I asked, looking up at the ceiling.

Johnnie and Ab both came out of the kitchen into the east room.

"Hell, Casey," Johnnie said with a grin, "you just lost a tooth and slipped a little hide. . . . How you doin'?"

"Great," I moaned. "But I ain't dancin' with that fat gal anymore."

Ab grinned, rolled a cigarette and handed it to me and then struck a match for me to light it on.

"Where'd y'all find me? *How'd* you find me while I was still alive?"

"We were out at the barn shoein' some horses," Johnnie said, "and we thought we heard a couple of gunshots. We got to watchin' and d'rectly seen a loose horse comin' down off that long ridge the other side of Trujillo Creek, so we figured we might ought to see about it. Come to find out, though, that it wasn't a loose horse we seen. Hell, it was your gray, and he wasn't loose at all because you had him roped right around the saddle horn."

"What was you doin'?" Ab asked. "Teachin' old gray how to pull?" Then we all laughed, and Johnnie reached inside the tarp of his bedroll and pulled out a little bottle of Rose Bud whiskey. After I'd taken a drink of it I said, "That just might be the best damn whiskey I ever drank. Thank you, fellers. I owe you. Sorry I whipped your butt yesterday, Johnnie," I said.

"You whipped *my* butt?" Johnnie said.

I stuck my tongue in the space where the bottom

tooth had been knocked out and smiled. Every time I moved or changed positions it hurt somewhere. "I don't recommend ever getting drug, fellers. I'll admit I was scared, scared as hell, and there wasn't a damn thing I could do. I thought I was dead, and I would have been if it hadn't been for you two."

"The way it looked you got drug about half a mile," Ab said, "but when we found you your gray was just walkin' along and not hurting you much, just dragging you through the grass. I guess he'd have killed you eventually, but most horses would have done it before we ever got a chance to cut you loose. . . . What 'n the hell happened?"

I thought about it a minute and said, "Gray fell with me and I got tangled up in my rope."

"Bullshit," Johnnie said. "We backtracked you and found the dead horse on top of the ridge—shot between the eyes. Stagg put your rope around your feet, didn't he?"

"It's my fight, boys," I told them.

"What happened?" Ab asked. "This got something to do with how you said you and Josh owed Stagg some money and you were going to pay him back and invite us to watch you whip his ass?"

I nodded, tonguing the empty space in my gum. "Didn't you get the invitation?"

"No," Johnnie said. "You're gonna have to do it all over again just so we can watch. I'm curious as hell. How about you, Ab?"

"It's my fight," I said again. "The son of a bitch the same as killed Josh and—"

"What!" Johnnie said.

"He set us up and stole cattle right from under our

noses and we got fired because of it. Y'all weren't involved, and you're not invited to the fight."

"What about Raven?" Johnnie hesitated a second and then said, "Okay . . . Lillie. What about Lillie? She involved in it?"

"The shooting you heard? Part of it was her tryin' to get Stagg and his men off me. The dead horse was the horse Stagg shot out from under her while she was holding a rifle on him."

Johnnie shook his head. "It don't make a whole lot of sense, Casey. What were you doing out there?"

"Tryin' to bring back the cattle Stagg stole while me and Josh were here. I was just goin' to throw 'em back onto the XIT. I thought it would make things right somehow. It was just something I felt like I had to do."

"And what about Lillie? What was she doin' out there?"

"I don't know for sure," I said.

"You said Stagg the same as killed Josh. How? I thought it was just a combination of getting hung up and hurt and then drinking too much whiskey."

"Stagg paid for the whiskey and he paid for the room," I said.

"But it wasn't like Josh to just hole up by himself and drink till he couldn't drink no more."

"It's *my* fight," I said again.

A light came on in Johnnie's eyes. "*She* was with Josh, wasn't she? She set you up, too, didn't she? Why?"

I shook my head. "Money, I guess."

"Sure," Johnnie said. "Whores'll do anything for money."

I looked at Johnnie. "I owe you, Johnnie—but just shut up about her."

"Okay, I'll shut up about her," he said. "We'll help you get the cattle back soon as you can ride."

"I told you that it's my fight, dammit! I'll do it alone."

"Hell, Casey," Ab said, "ol' Josh was our friend too, you know. We'll help you get the cattle."

"It's not just about the cattle now," I said.

"What else is it about?"

"Revenge?" Johnnie asked. "You tryin' to show Tatum Stagg what a tough bastard you are?"

"No!" I snapped. "I've got to get Lillie out of there!"

"You've got to do what? You're gonna get yourself killed over a whore who set you up and got you fired, who you just said had a hand in Josh's death? I thought you had more sense than that, Casey."

"Well, that proves you don't know much, I guess, don't it!" I told Johnnie. "I *don't* have any more sense than that!"

"Casey, come on! It's one thing to be fooled by a pretty woman when you don't know anything about her, but—"

"I thought you said you were going to shut up about her?" I said. "I ain't askin' you to come—I wouldn't even *let* you come if you wanted to. This is between me and Stagg."

"Well, you're damn right it is if you're talking about going up against Tatum Stagg to get that woman away from him. Ain't that right, Ab?"

"Aw, come on, Johnnie," Ab said, "why don't you tell him?"

I looked at Ab and then at Johnnie. "Tell me what?"

"Aw, shit, Ab!" Johnnie moaned. "Just when he was getting stirred up enough so he was fun to watch, too."

"What, dammit!" I said.

"She came by here this afternoon," Ab said.

"Who did? Lillie?"

Ab nodded, and Johnnie held his hands in the air and then slapped himself on the legs. "Spill your guts, Deacons!" he said. "He won't be any fun now."

"Lillie was here!" I said. "Today?"

"Just about sundown," Ab said. "She was crying. Said you'd gotten drug by your horse and wanted us to help her find you. We told her you were here and not in too bad of shape either."

"Then what?" I asked.

"Then she thanked us and left before we could even ask her what happened to you."

"You just let her go?"

"Yeah, we let her go," Johnnie said. "There wasn't anything else we could do other than maybe kidnap her and tie her up out in the barn."

"I wonder how . . . ," I said, thinking. "How'd she look?"

Ab and Johnnie looked at each other, and then Ab said, "The best we could tell she looked like hell, Casey. She never got very close, and she kept her head down most of the time. But her face was bruised and puffy. She said she fell."

"That dirty bastard," I whispered.

"Stagg?" Ab said.

"Yeah," I said. "Stagg. I'd better go find her."

"Hell, Casey," Johnnie said, "I'll bet she's back in Tascosa at the Exchange Saloon by now wearin' a red satin dress and black stockin's just like she was the first time I saw her, and I'll bet that you or Stagg neither one are layin' very heavy on her mind. The best I remember, she never had trouble finding some old boy to entertain her."

I stood up slow and stiff and painful. "I don't feel like hittin' you right now, Johnnie," I said. "Don't get me wrong, I *want* to hit you and hit you hard, but I just don't feel like it. Where's my boots?"

"Good gawd!" Johnnie said. "You can't even walk! How in the hell are you going to saddle your horse?"

I looked at the two of them. "I can do it," I said.

"I'll saddle your damn horse for you, Casey," Ab said.

I smiled and looked at Johnnie. "You should try being more like Ab, Johnnie. You see how he just offered his assistance without being rude or crude or runnin' off at the mouth?"

"Just because Ab's got a special weakness for cripples and chowderheads don't mean he's some kind of saint," Johnnie said as he tossed my boots onto the bedroll.

"Thanks," I said, struggling to get into my boots.

CHAPTER
20

I smelled the cedar smoke coming from the little rock cabin beside the Blue Hole in Rana Canyon before I got to the canyon's rim. I had dreamed of riding in at dark, tired and weary, and smelling the smoke coming from that cabin, or at least one very much like it, and knowing that Lillie was there waiting for me. But, even though it was happening, things were different now, much different. There was a wall now between me and Lillie, a wall put there by the events of the past couple of days.

I'd left Trujillo Camp underneath a blanket of twinkling stars, but during the ride those stars had disappeared behind a heavy blanket of clouds. By the time I got to the rim of the canyon, there was a cold wind blowing from the north, and occasionally I could feel a hard pellet of snow hit my face.

Once I found the trail that led from the rimrock to the canyon's floor, which in the dark was no nester's picnic, I hobbled my horse beside Lillie's and limped to the cabin. When I stepped through the rock doorway into the flickering yellow light of the small cedar-wood fire, I saw Lillie. She was standing on the far side of the little room pointing a rifle at the doorway. She was wearing a blue riding skirt and a plaid wool jacket. Her long black hair was a mess. Her face was a mess, too. It was puffy and bruised. One eye was black, and both of them were red from crying. Her cheeks were dirty where she had been wiping away tears.

We looked at each other for a few silent seconds before she lowered the rifle.

I limped to the fire, threw in a few more sticks and poured myself a cup of the coffee she had boiled. Then I sat down on my bedroll and rolled a smoke without saying a word. After I'd lit the cigarette, Lillie sat on the ground close to the fire hugging her knees and watching the flames.

The new cedar sticks popped as they caught fire, and that was practically the only sound in the cabin. Whatever other sound there might have been, it sure wasn't people talking.

Another cup of coffee and I went outside to unsaddle the horses. It was snowing harder, and the wind was moaning through the cedars on the rimrock overhead. I carried the saddles inside and made three trips for wood. When I came in with the last of the wood, Lillie was asleep on the ground beside the fire.

I threw the tarp and the blankets back on my bedroll, picked Lillie up without waking her, laid her in the bedroll and covered her up. Then I put more wood on the fire, made myself a bed out of the saddle blankets and laid my weary body down beside the fire.

The next thing I knew the fire had died out and I

was cold. Looking out the open doorway I could see a little daylight starting to seep down into Rana Canyon from the rim above. I could also see snow falling into the canyon. Not little hard pellets of snow like had hit me on the face last night, but flakes about the size of my thumbnail and falling so thick I could see no farther downcanyon than a man could have shot a deer with a good rifle.

I walked to the door and looked out. The horses were still hobbled and had turned their butts to the north. Their heads were down and their backs were covered with snow, but they were okay—they weren't wet and they weren't shivering.

I built the fire back up, and the coffee had just come to a boil when Lillie sat up in my bedroll. She looked outside and spoke the first words either of us had spoken since I stepped into the cabin the night before and saw her holding the rifle. She said, "That's beautiful!" and her eyes sparkled and she seemed to have, for the moment at least, forgotten her bruises and bumps and the wall that circumstances had built between us.

"Yeah, it sure is beautiful," I said. "There's nothing like a little cow-country canyon in a quiet snowfall where the snow just piles up on the cedar branches and the rocks. It's about the most peaceful thing in the world. People who don't know, think cowboys are in that line of work for the excitement, but really it's the peace and quiet in between the excitin' times that mean the most to most of us."

"That's a strange thing for a cowboy to say," Lillie said.

I shrugged. "Most of 'em won't ever say it, especially when they're in a saloon drinking fightin'-andbraggin' whiskey." I thought about how that sounded and said on the heels of it, "I didn't mean that the only time you talked to cowboys was—"

"It's okay, Casey," Lillie said. "For the most part, that's true—that *is* about the only time I ever talked to cowboys. There's no need hiding or avoiding the truth about ourselves, Casey. We are what we are."

"Just like Stagg said, huh?"

"At times he can be very truthful, in spite of what else he is. What he said about us—about me and him—was true."

"But why?" I asked, just like I'd asked myself a hundred times. "You're beautiful and smart and—"

"And full of fear and self-pity. Too ready to make excuses for myself for past mistakes so the future mistakes would be easier to live with. Sometimes people are too ready to take whatever life gives them as though it's what they deserve; they lack the courage to say they won't accept it. They don't have the courage to refuse to participate in a lowly existence. They don't have the strength to stand up to life and demand a better fate. Everybody isn't brave and strong and sure of themselves like you are, Casey. Some of us are weak and afraid and unsure."

I had to laugh at that. Sometimes I wasn't even sure which horse to catch at night for the next morning's work, but I didn't tell Lillie. I said, "Maybe Stagg's the one who's strong and brave and sure of himself. He knows what he wants and he goes out and takes it. He has everything, seems like. His own place, his own cattle . . . his own woman."

Lillie looked up at me with the hurt showing in her eyes again, but she didn't say anything, didn't try to defend herself.

"Why'd you pull that rifle on him to try to stop him from whipping me?" I said. "That was a stupid thing to do."

Lillie looked out the door at the falling snow for a long time without speaking or moving. Finally she said, "Because I didn't want you to get hurt."

I shrugged my shoulders. "Why not?" I said. "What difference would that make to you? Me and Josh are just a couple of nobody cowboys, aren't we? The plan was to use us to get what you wanted. Isn't that right? What's the difference if we get hurt in the process? Besides, the damage is just about complete anyway. Josh died, and you've already hurt me more on the inside than Stagg can ever hurt me on the outside, even if he drags off all my hide."

"And now you really want to hurt *me*, don't you, Casey?" Lillie said softly. "How can I blame you?" She stood up and stepped toward the saddles lying in the corner of the shack. "I'll saddle my horse and be going."

She picked up her bridle and turned toward me. "I'll not bother you with excuses for what I've done or what I have—what I *had*—become. But you treated me with respect that night at Trujillo Camp and all the next day—respect I hadn't known for a long time. I saw goodness and decency in you, and when I did I saw how far down I'd let myself be dragged. I know I hurt you and I'm sorry. I'm sorry about all of it. But I'm different now, thanks to you. You asked why I pulled a rifle on Tatum, and I said it was because I didn't want to see you get hurt—and that was the truth. But I would have tried to stop him no matter who it had been because it was the right thing to do. When I saw the hate in Tatum's eyes I realized all of a sudden what there is about you that infuriates him. It's integrity—you have it and he doesn't.''

Suddenly Lillie's high opinion of me was beginning to make me feel a little uncomfortable. After all, I did have my own blemished past to contend with. "Well," I said, "I wouldn't say—"

"Tatum couldn't buy your integrity from you, and he can't take it away from you no matter what he does. I realized something else, Casey—the only way anybody loses their integrity is by giving it away. I lost mine somewhere along the way, and I've been accusing other people of taking it away from me, but they didn't. *I gave it away!* And now I'm trying to find it again." Then she picked up her saddle and struggled with it toward the door. She looked small and weak—and yet she seemed incredibly strong, too.

"Lillie," I said. She turned around as she got to the doorway and looked at me. "It's snowing awful hard out there."

She turned to look outside again.

"Look—you can't hardly even see!" I said. "And the wind's probably drifting the snow once you get out of the canyon. Your tracks would be gone in a few minutes and you couldn't even tell where you'd been. It's awful hard to keep from losing your directions when it's snowing like it is now. Only a fool would be out . . . in . . . that." A sudden, foolish thought popped into my head.

"What?" Lillie said.

"Nothing." But the thought wouldn't leave my head, and I couldn't stop looking outside at the snow.

"What is it, Casey?"

I shrugged and turned away from the door.

"Nothing. . . . It's just too bad for *you* to be out, that's all."

"The cows!" Lillie said. "You're thinking about going back to Tatum's place and getting those cows again *in this snow!*"

"No! That would be stupid!" I said, wondering how she knew what I was thinking.

Lillie dropped her saddle and crossed the grassy floor of the cabin to me, her puffy, red eyes now lit with eagerness. "But that's why it might work, isn't it!"

"Stagg would *never* think of me coming back in this," I admitted. "Besides, he probably thinks I'm dead."

"And he would never think that I'd have the nerve to help you, even if I could."

"You?" I almost yelled it out.

"Yes . . . me!" she said excitedly. "I'll help you!"

"But, Lillie, you can't . . . Johnnie and Ab will help me."

Lillie grabbed my arm. "Oh, Casey, please let me help you. Don't you see that I have to do this! Please!"

"Lillie, you can't. . . . It'll be too cold for you, and I can't promise that I won't get lost myself. A man could freeze to death out there if this turns into a real blizzard."

"Casey, why is it so important to you to take those cows back to the XIT?"

"Well," I said, trying to think how I could explain it so it would make sense to her, "it's just the principle of the thing. It's just something I've got to do."

"Exactly!" Lillie said with the passion of the firmest conviction I'd witnessed in a long time. "Do you think life is more important to me for some reason than it is to you, and my principles *less* important? Look at us! Beat up and skinned up! Black and blue! Both of us, so sore it hurts to move! Tatum used both of us! But this isn't for revenge, because even if we knew he was dead we would still feel like we had to take those cows back to the XIT. I'll do it alone if I have to. Maybe I *should* do it alone." And she moved again toward the door.

This was not a job for a woman; it didn't take much to see that. It would be cold and miserable and dangerous. I grabbed her by the arm and spun her around. "No. . . . *I'll* do it!" I said. "You stay here where it's warm; you'll just be in my way. Besides, I'd *rather* do it alone."

"You self-righteous bastard!" she said. She started crying again. "Do you hate me so much that you'd take this chance away from me? You get to come back, feeling good about yourself and—"

She was so mad she hit me in the chest with the bottom of a clinched fist. I grabbed her hands, and the next thing I knew I was pulling her into me and kissing her. It wasn't anything I had planned on doing, but just the same I *was* doing it. But unlike the time on the porch at Endee when she kissed me back and made it just about the sweetest and warmest thing I'd ever known, now she didn't kiss me back at all. She didn't fight or pull away, but she didn't kiss back either.

I looked down at her and let her go. "Kind of embarrassing," I said, "when two people are kissing but one's not."

"I'm sorry, Casey," she said softly. "It's just that

I'm not sure who you're kissing now, me or Raven. I don't even think you know for sure."

"Sure I do," I said.

"Then who were you trying to kiss, Casey? Was it the whore or the sweet and innocent one?"

For an embarrassing moment I was unable to speak.

"You see," Lillie said, "you *don't* know, do you? But I don't blame you, Casey. I guess the truth is *I'm* not even sure who I am anymore. I would like to think that the real me is somewhere in between the woman Tatum knows and the woman you thought you fell in love with, but, you see, I'm not even sure who I am. . . . But you could help me find out, Casey. You could help me find out what I'm capable of. What is it you men say? You could help me find out what I'm really made of."

"Aw, hell, Lillie," I said. "I think you're makin' a bigger deal over gettin' those cows back than it really is."

She smiled. "And I think you are, too, Casey. After all, it's not going to change the world, is it? But, what the hell, let's give it a shot anyway."

"No," I said.

"You want to go out and slay the giant and come back and claim the girl, huh?"

I looked at her funny. What she said sounded good to me, but somehow I sensed she felt differently about it.

"So in a way, I'll be one of the fruits of victory—or the spoils of war, huh?" she went on. "And if Tatum comes back instead of you, then *he'll* get me, right? And if neither of you comes for me, I'll wait until some other man comes. Right, Casey? Well, no thanks!" Without me realizing it, she had been moving slowly toward the spot where the rifle she had been holding when I came in the night before was leaning against the rock wall. Suddenly she reached for it, and suddenly it was pointed at my middle again. "I'll fight my own battles from here on and choose for myself who I'll be with or even *if* I'll be with anybody."

I looked at Lillie a long time and then let out a sigh and moved toward the saddles.

"What are you going to do?" she asked.

"I'm goin' to saddle the horses," I said. "That is, unless you want to go to Tatum's place and then drive those cows all the way to Texas afoot—and if you have that in mind, then *I'll* be here where it's safe and warm waitin' on you. If you don't mind, maybe you ought to pull all the blankets out of my bedroll for us to take along with us."

As I carried the saddles out the door Lillie said, "Casey." I stopped and turned around, and she said, "Thanks."

I smiled. "Thank the Winchester," I said. "But just remember I warned you that this ain't going to be any nester's picnic."

CHAPTER
21

When I had saddled the horses, me and Lillie had a short argument, after which she agreed to let me refashion her outfit and make it more suitable for punching cows in a snowstorm. The first thing I did was to dig a pair of my britches out of my bedroll and tell her to put them on over her riding skirt. After that I put a blanket over her coat, making her a hood and tying it at the neck and waist with two short pieces of rope. Then I figured we were ready to go.

From the Blue Hole, Rana Canyon angled toward the southwest, and we stayed in it as long as we could. It was snowing hard when we rode away from the cabin, but the canyon's walls protected us from the wind and we could enjoy how peaceful it made the canyon. The snow settled softly and quietly on everything, from my hat and Lillie's hood to the cedar boughs and fall-cured grass. Rabbits and quail skitted in silence from bush to bush, and a big mule deer buck only raised his head and watched us cautiously as we rode by within fifty feet of him.

We weren't in the canyon for more than a mile or so, but of all the thousands of miles I'd ridden before and all I've ridden since, I remember the single mile in Rana Canyon better than just about any other. The horse Lillie was riding was a black horse without a white hair on him. The blanket that covered her from head to foot was brown. The eyes that looked out from underneath the hood formed by that brown blanket were black and sparkling like obsidian. The face was happy and smiling and, even with the black eye, more beautiful than anything I'd ever seen before.

There was something primitive in the way Lillie looked and in the way I felt—like we were an Indian warrior and his squaw going to battle. Yet there was something gentle, too, like the snowflakes hitting my face. And something strong and good that I could feel as we rode between the walls of Rana Canyon, but the nearest I can come to explaining it is by just saying the world felt like a good, strong, well-broke horse feels under the saddle.

But on top of everything else, on top of the primitive, the gentle, the strong and the good, I felt a touch of the melancholy, and that was because I knew the good times never last long enough. Every trail sooner or later leaves the canyon floor and climbs to the rimrock, and before our trail did that I wanted to stop and hold Lillie in my arms and tell her I didn't give a damn about a woman named Raven and that I gave even less of a damn about Tatum Stagg and thirty-three head of XIT cows.

So I pulled to a stop and tried to say what I was feeling inside, but it didn't come out exactly like I wanted it to. "I was goin' to ask you to marry me, you know," I said. "I had it all planned out for us. I was going to settle down and file on a homestead and—"

"And now you're trying to show me what a good deal I missed out on by not being the woman I should have been, is that right, Casey? Of course, it never dawned on you that I just might not have *wanted* to marry you! I said you were a decent man who treated me with respect, but that doesn't mean I wanted to have your babies. If I have any regrets, and I do, missing out on the chance to be Mrs. Casey Wills so I could grow old and wrinkled on some godforsaken homestead is not one of them!" Then she slapped the black on the rump with her bridle reins and started him up the trail that would lead us out of Rana Canyon.

"Well, I'll be . . . ," I said through my gritted teeth. "I liked you a hell of a lot better before you started worryin' about your damn integrity! I wouldn't have you now on a bet! No sir, not on a bet! Just like I wouldn't have a homestead. You didn't think I was serious about that, did you? What would I do with one of those damn things? I'm a cowboy, a big-outfit cowboy, not a mare-ridin', white-bread-eatin' nester of a homesteader who'd let some woman lead him around by the nose. Look at you! You don't even have the cowboy courtesy not to ride in front of the segundo!"

Lillie stopped halfway up the snow-covered trail and looked back at me, maybe to apologize or maybe to cry some more, I didn't know which. After all, I'd put her in her place pretty damn good, which, being a man and all, I figured was my rightful duty. But Lillie didn't do either of the things I figured she might.

Instead, she smiled pretty, which is an unfair advantage God has given women over men, and said, "Who made you the segundo anyway?"

"God did," I said. "That's who! It's in the Bible."

Lillie laughed, and when Lillie laughed I couldn't help but smile. When I got to the top of the trail and stopped beside her on top of the rimrock she said, "Look—it's not much windier up here than it was down in the canyon."

She was right about the wind—there was only a north breeze to give a small slant to the big snowflakes as they fell to the ground. Still, I had a feeling something bad was going to happen. Maybe it was because Lillie looked even smaller and more fragile once we were on top of the rimrock than she had down in the canyon. The canyon seemed to be a small world all to itself where peace and harmony ruled, isolated from the rest of the world and nestled safely between two steep walls. But the world on top of the rimrock was a big world stretching mile upon mile in every direction, and there was nothing to stop the cold north wind once it began to blow.

"I think we ought to turn back," I said.

"Why?" Lillie asked.

"I've just got a feeling we should. This was a crazy idea. I never should have let you talk me into it to start with. Let's go back."

"No!" Lillie yelled. "We're not turning back! It's not any colder up here than it was in the canyon. Let's go!" Then she slapped her black horse on the rump again and took off across the snow in a lope.

"Damn!" I said and shook my head. "Stupid, hardheaded little . . ."

I caught up with her and yelled, "Wait a minute, dammit!"

She stopped the black.

"What'll you do if *I* go back?" I asked. "You'd be lost in ten minutes out here by yourself. You couldn't even find that prissy bottom of yours with both hands! You're a . . . a dreamer!"

She looked flabbergasted. "I'm a dreamer?" she almost yelled, laying a hand on her chest. "You're the dreamer! You had this grand illusion about what you *thought* I was—what you wanted me to be—that had nothing to do with what I really was. And now you're mad at me because I don't fit *your* dream anymore. Well, next time you might just ask the woman you're dreaming about if she'd care to be in your . . . your . . . your damn stupid dream!"

"You're not part of my dream—you're part of my nightmare!" I said. "What man in his right mind would ever dream of bein' cooped up in a little canyon cabin with you! If I want a whore, I'll take a couple of dollars to town and buy me one, but I sure as hell wouldn't ever marry one!"

Well, that did it. Lillie started crying again, even though I could tell she was trying real hard not to. But I could see the hurt and the tears welling up inside her, and pretty soon they started coming out, not fast and loud the way I'd seen some women bawl, but slow and silent and, God, I think those tears hurt me as much as what I'd said hurt her. I hated myself for what I'd said.

"I'm sorry, Lillie," I said. "I didn't mean that." I looked at her for a few seconds and then said, "Aw hell, let's go." Then I headed toward the southwest, toward Tatum Stagg's place.

After I'd trotted about fifty yards, I glanced back and saw that Lillie was not following me. I pulled up and twisted around in the saddle to see her better. "Are you comin'?" I said.

"Do you want me to?" she asked.

"Guess so," I said.

"Why?" she asked.

"Because," I said with a shrug.

"Because why?"

I thought for a minute and then said, "Because it seems like if we're both going to Stagg's place, we might just as well ride together."

"Is that the only reason?"

Another reason I could think of was what I'd already told her about her not being able to find her prissy bottom with both hands, but I held off saying it again. Instead, I said, "Maybe we can help each other when we get there."

"Is that all?" she asked.

"Well . . . ain't that enough?"

"It would have been nice if you'd said you enjoyed my company," she said.

I looked straight up into the air and blew out all the air I had in my lungs. Then I said, "Well, *of course* I enjoy your company. What man in his right mind wouldn't? What man—" But then I stopped myself. I was afraid to say any more along those lines at all. Every time I did, my mouth said something the rest of me didn't really mean.

We sat on our horses fifty snow-filled yards apart for a few seconds looking at each other. Finally Lillie spurred her horse forward. I waited, this time, until she was alongside me before I struck a trot. After we'd covered a couple of wordless miles, I looked at her and said, "Cold?"

Lillie shook her head but didn't answer otherwise.

"It's a good thing," I said. "It's probably not much below freezing now, but it'll be a lot colder by the time we get through. We haven't gone too far to turn back, not yet anyway."

"So turn back," she said. "I won't hold it against you."

I grinned and shook my head. "I wonder how long we would have lasted."

"Doing what?" she asked.

"Being married—livin' under the same roof and sharin' the same bed?"

Lillie was the one who smiled now. "You're the one who had the dream—you tell me."

CHAPTER
22

Look familiar?" I asked, watching Lillie as I lifted the reins to stop the gray at the southern edge of a small mesa. Below us, at the foot of the mesa, was Tatum Stagg's place, his big set of pole corrals, his barn, his house. Up on the mesa where we sat on our horses it was cold, but it was only barely snowing and the wind was only blowing a little harder than it had been when we rode out of Rana Canyon two hours earlier. Down below, smoke was coming from Stagg's rock chimney. "Stagg's probably got his house all nice and warm, just waitin' for you to come back," I said.

Lillie shrugged. "He probably does. He thinks that no matter what he does to me, I'll always come back to him."

"You always did before, didn't you?"

Lillie nodded.

"I guess you spent a lot of time in that house, huh?"

"Way *too* much time."

"Lots of nights?"

Lillie looked at me. Finally, she said, "Yeah—a *lot* of nights, damn it! Do you want me to tell you what we did?"

"No need to," I said. "It don't take much imagination to figure he wasn't just payin' you to cook and wash dishes—or to sit out on the porch and sing hymns with him after supper. What I *don't* know is this—did you do it just for the money?"

"No," Lillie answered slowly, sadly, "it wasn't just for the money. There were times when I could almost convince myself that Tatum really cared for me. . . . It wasn't like he put a few dollars on the bed stand every time, Casey. As a matter of fact, he never just outright gave me money. He bought me things and—"

"And paid for your hotel room," I said. "I've been wondering—how many other XIT cowboys did you have up to room two twelve, trying to convince them to turn their heads while Stagg stole cattle from the outfit? Surely old Josh wasn't the first—he was just the first one to die there. Right?"

"Somehow I thought you were different from Tatum," Lillie said. "But the more I'm with you the less difference I can see."

She spurred her horse straight toward the mesa's rimrock, but I reached out and grabbed one of her bridle reins and jerked the black to a stop.

"What 'n the hell do you think you're doin'?" I said.

"What we came here to do! There's cows down there in the corrals and—"

"And you might just as well string a telegraph line to Stagg's front room and tell him all about what we're planning as ride off the rim right above his house! Whether you like it or not, you're going to do what I say! Hell, I guess to you anything that wears hair, walks on four legs, eats grass and bellers is a cow. . . . Well, for your information those aren't cows down there in the corrals, they're yearlin's. What we want to find is the same thirty-three head of cows that Stagg took while me and Josh were livin' at Trujillo Camp! *They're* the ones we need to shore up our integrities. Remember?"

Lillie glared at me but then reluctantly said, "Okay . . . but let's do it! Let's find the cows and get them back to Texas as fast as we can so I can get away from here—and away from you and Tatum both!"

"Suits me," I said as I reined the gray away from the rimrock.

We pulled back from the southern rim of the mesa and in a few minutes were at the top of a steep trail on the west side, above Revuelto Creek.

Just before I started off the trail, I twisted around in my saddle and said to Lillie, "Let me get at least halfway down before you start off. It'll be slippery, but just give your horse his head and let him take his time."

I don't remember the particulars of the story, if there were any, but I remember hearing Josh say one time that a man could always tell a woman . . . but he couldn't tell her much. Well, there was more common sense in that statement than just about anything else I ever heard Josh say.

Before it could be said that me and the gray had even had a good start down the trail, I heard a racket behind me and looked back to see Lillie and her black coming off the rim, too, which was not a welcome sight since the trail was slick because of four inches of wet snow. And underneath the snow, but hard to see, were pieces of shale rock, some as small as a spur rowel and some as big as a saddle blanket. And also, to make the trail all the slicker, in some places the ground underneath the snow and the shale would be frozen and in some places it would be thawed.

It wasn't a tall mesa we were coming off of like a man would find farther west and closer to the eastern slope of the Rockies but one of the shorter, smaller ones like are found on a cow-country prairie. The trail from rimrock to the foot of the mesa was probably no more than three hundred feet all told, with two smooth switchbacks in it—ordinarily no trouble at all for a horse to come down, but the snow, not to mention Lillie, made it no ordinary coming-off-the-mesa excursion.

With Lillie as close behind me as she was, I decided, instead of giving her any more instructions she could totally disregard, I'd just hold my breath and *hope* we'd both get to the bottom of the trail without getting either of the horses down.

Things were fine until we were three-fourths of the way down, then her horse slipped a little. She panicked and jerked on the reins, trying to stop the sliding horse. The horse threw his head up when the curb pinched him, which meant he couldn't see the ground; he stepped sideways where he should have stepped straight ahead; Lillie jerked on him again, this time trying to turn him around and go back *up* the trail. When she tried that particular maneuver, all four feet slipped out from underneath the black, and before I could say the words befitting such a circumstance, she and the black were underneath me and the gray. Then we all went to the bottom of the mesa in one hell of a tangled heap.

When we stopped sliding at the bottom of the mesa, the horses kicked and flounced until they got their feet underneath them again and stood up. Still sitting flat on the ground, I wiped the snow out of my eyes and saw that neither of the horses was carrying a leg—they were just standing around looking bewildered.

I looked for Lillie. She was just sitting up. The blanket-poncho she was wearing was over her head, and she was fighting to get it off. I didn't say nothing until she had her head clear. Then I looked at her and said, "Good gawd, how stupid can you be?" and put my hat on, not knowing it was full of snow.

I wiped the snow off my face again and then cleaned it all out of my hat. When I put my hat back on, I looked at Lillie and said, "Why in the hell didn't you——" But she was starting to laugh so I stopped. Her laugh wasn't loud at first, but it kept getting louder and louder.

"You can laugh if you want to," I said, still sitting on the ground, "but it's just a goddamn wonder we weren't both killed. . . . If you were a man I'd whip your butt!"

"Would you turn your hat around and get the horseshit off the top of it first?" she said and then fell back in the snow, laughing again.

I took my hat off and looked. It *had* been on backwards, and there *was* a horse apple stuck in the crease on top. "No," I said, getting to my knees and moving toward Lillie, strangely feeling a little drunk, "I'm gonna whip your butt."

Lillie stopped laughing. "You mean *if* I was a man."

"No," I said, reaching for her, "that ain't what I mean at all."

She scrambled to get away from me, but I grabbed her foot and pulled her back to me over the snow like a sled until she was right in front of me on her stomach. I swatted her butt and said, "That's what I mean!" with a chuckle.

"Ouch . . . You . . . ," she yelled, rolling over and grabbing my hand. I tried to twist my hand free but, for as little as she was, she had a good grip. I pulled and she pulled and then I guess I slipped on the snow and fell on top of her.

For a second we were like two people frozen in the snow, with our noses nearly touching but neither one of us doing anything other than breathing, and not doing much of that, just looking into each other's eyes. Then suddenly we weren't just staring—we were kissing. And, if our bodies had been frozen a second earlier, they sure started thawing out in a hurry.

She twisted her head, and our lips came apart. I kissed her hair and kissed her ear and I kissed her in the hollow of her throat.

"Casey . . . I need time," she whispered. "I've got to be sure you know who you're kissing. You've got to be sure who—"

My lips found hers again and . . .

From behind me, someone said, "Casey? What 'n the hell? Are you awright? Well . . . good gawd! Whadaya think they're doin', Ab?"

I rolled off Lillie and looked up to see Johnnie Lester and Ab Deacons sitting on their horses a little ways up the trail me and Lillie had just slid down. They were looking down at us and smiling.

"I don't know," Ab said. "Maybe they're toothin' each other—tryin' to find out how old they are."

"Or maybe she's got a chicken bone stuck in her throat," Johnnie said with a wink and a giggle. "Y'all ain't been eatin' chicken, have you, Casey?"

I stood up and brushed the snow off my chaps and coat and pulled my hat down on my head. "Our horses slipped comin' down the trail," I growled.

"Funny," Johnnie said, *"we* didn't have any trouble."

"You didn't have Lillie with you either," I said. "What're y'all doin' out here anyway? Looks like two big-outfit twisters like you'd have plenty to do on the other side of the fence. Mr. Findlay know you're not on the outfit?"

Johnnie smiled and then said, "We got to thinkin' about it this mornin'—I mean about what all you told us about Stagg and how he was responsible for Josh's dyin' and gettin' both of you fired and—"

"I said I didn't want your help," I said. "Don't you remember that? Don't you think I can drive a few head of cows a few miles by myself?" Suddenly I realized, listening to myself talk, how much I sounded like Josh. In a way, it scared me.

"We figured you *might* could do it—if you weren't all stove up from that draggin'," Johnnie said. "But we knew you were, and we knew today, with this snow, would be a good time to do it."

"That's what *we* came to do," Lillie said as she stood up and brushed the snow off her clothes.

"We?" Johnnie said, and then him and Ab looked at each other.

Lillie limped over to her horse, gathered up the black's reins and got on. When she settled in the saddle, she looked at the three of us and said, "What is it you cowboys say? 'Let's rattle our hocks, boys.'"

For several seconds the three of us, me and Johnnie and Ab, watched in silence as Lillie trotted slowly away from us. Then Johnnie said softly, sort of in a whisper, "Good gawdamighty damn."

I looked up at Johnnie—I still hadn't got on the gray but was standing in front of him holding the reins. I said, "Yeah."

"Why are you grinnin', Casey?" Johnnie asked.

I stepped on the gray, pitched him some slack in the reins and touched him with a spur. "Damned if I know," I said.

CHAPTER
23

Stagg had a fenced trap about a mile square down next to the creek. It was a little ways south of the house and on the other side of a low ridge from it. In that trap were thirty-two head of cows, many of which I recognized as being the ones I'd headed toward the XIT on my first try. The cow that wasn't there was the one who'd stayed in front before and was in a hurry to get back to Texas and find her calf. No doubt she'd given up on me rescuing her and had decided to take matters into her own hands and go back to Texas alone.

It wasn't exactly in a daring raid that we swooped down from the hills and got the cows. We just trotted up, threw the gate back and drove those cows out like we owned the place. Then Johnnie and Ab pointed the little herd east, toward Trujillo Camp, while me and Lillie kept the drags pushed up.

It was sometime not long past noon when we started east. Of course there was no sun to be seen overhead in the sky, just low, gray clouds and light snow. The wind was still no more than a breeze out of the north, but it was a cold breeze. My ears tingled and my toes were cold, but when a man lives almost his entire life outside, he reaches a point where he can take the cold and the ache it brings with it more or less in stride. It's all part of punching cows. That's only up to a point, of course, and a cowboy knows that in wintertime the cold that is usually no more than a tease can become his tormentor and deadliest enemy. On the plains, where any type of windbreak or shelter may be miles away, a man must be doubly wary of what's coming at him from the north. In the twenty-odd miles between Revuelto Creek, where Stagg's place was located, and Trujillo Camp, there was probably not a single bluff tall enough to offer a man a windbreak. The weather was holding, or seemed to be, and we had seen no sign, yet, of Stagg's bunch.

Still, I was uneasy—not for me or Ab or Johnnie. But Lillie was a woman, and it is a man's duty and responsibility to protect a woman. Even if I had hated Lillie, which I sure didn't, and even if I had never felt her sweet kisses or felt her body respond to my embrace, which I had, I would still have considered it my duty and obligation to protect her from dangers, both human and natural.

But our liberation of XIT beef was going better than I could have hoped when we rode out of Rana Canyon. Not only was the weather holding to an ear-tingling and a toe-aching chill, but Stagg had so far just as well have been in China. On top of both of those things, Johnnie and Ab were there, which I sure didn't resent anywhere near as much as I'd pretended to. As a matter of fact, I was damn glad they were there, because I knew what kind of men they were, and I knew, regardless of however they might feel about Lillie, they would feel as obligated as I did about protecting and defending her.

The cows strung out in a long walk toward Texas, and we pushed on in silence and without incident for five, ten miles. Me and Johnnie and Ab had driven cattle many times in the cold and the snow, so it was nothing new to us, no more than part of another day's work, except for the circumstances of course. But it was new to Lillie, all of it was, being horseback in the cold and the snow, driving cattle in it. Still, she sat in the saddle as straight and stoic as any of us.

We pushed on across another five miles of snow-covered rolling hills and sagebrush. The cows were now walking slower. No cows in that country carried any extra flesh to speak of through the winter, and very few would have been strong to begin with. On top of that it had only been yesterday that I had driven them to within a few miles of the Texas fence before Stagg intercepted me and drove them back to his place. Now they had come many miles *again,* and most of them were springing—carrying calves in their wombs—which only made traveling for them more difficult.

"I bet they wish we and Stagg would settle our differences and quit drivin' them back and forth," I said to Lillie, practically the first words I'd said since we left the trap at Stagg's place.

Lillie turned her head toward me for a second but didn't say anything.

"You cold?" I asked.

"I'll make it," she answered.

A mile or so later I felt the wind change directions, from the north to the northeast. The wind was colder, too—a lot colder. Johnnie looked back at me, and I looked over at Lillie, who now, instead of looking straight ahead like she had done since leaving Stagg's place, had her head ducked against the wind.

I yelled at the cows now and slapped my chaps to booger them into traveling faster. I wanted them to hit a short trot, but a little faster walk was all they were willing to give me, even when I took my rope down and started popping it against my chap leg. I whipped a couple of them on the butt, but I could tell they were not going to go any faster into the wind and the snow, which was now swirling into their faces, just like it was ours. It was impossible to tell if it was snowing harder or if it was just the wind picking the powdery snow up off the ground—not that it really mattered which it was.

The good news was that the wind would cover our tracks—as if Stagg would need to read tracks to know what had become of the latest acquisition to his herd.

We kept pushing on, but the pushing was harder now, harder for all of us—cows, horses and people. Me and Johnnie and Ab took our neckerchiefs from around our necks and put them over our heads and around our ears and then put our hats back on. There was nothing we could do for our toes except to get off and walk, but we would have been walking in several inches of snow, so we stayed in our saddles.

I rode up beside Lillie and asked, "How are you doin'?"

She nodded her head.

"Are you cold?" I asked.

She looked at me for a second like I was crazy and

then nodded her head again. She had the blanket pulled up so I could only see her eyes.

"You should have stayed at the cabin!"

Lillie quickly shook her head. Shook it several times and then pointed toward the east.

"We've got about five miles to go yet," I said. "I just hope these cows don't plumb quit us. . . . Lillie, it's okay to be cold. I'm cold. Johnnie's cold. Ab's cold. The whole world is cold. Maybe me and you should trot on ahead and get the fire and coffee ready for Johnnie and Ab at Trujillo Camp."

Lillie shook her head, and we pushed on, still slower it seemed to me, into the blowing snow.

It began turning dark. And then it was dark, but not really, not with the whiteness of the snow. But it was night. I could still see about as far as I could before the gray day turned to a white night, which meant I could see Johnnie and Ab on each side of the herd, and sometimes I could see the front of the herd. I think all of us were using the wind to keep our bearings. As long as it was hitting us on the left front, we should be traveling east.

How much farther could it be? A mile? Two miles? The landmarks that should have answered no longer existed. Where was Trujillo Creek? We would have to cross it a mile or so before we hit the fence—that is, *if* we were going straight.

I rode close to Lillie and said, "Let's get off and walk before we frostbite our toes." When my toes stopped aching, I knew that walking in the snow was the least of two evils.

While I held the reins of Lillie's horse, I stomped my feet in the snow. At first I could feel nothing, but in a few seconds the pain returned.

Lillie stepped off and collapsed. "I . . . I don't know if I *can* walk, Casey," she said softly.

I laid a hand at the top of her left boot. Something felt strange. I slid off my glove and pulled up the leg of the pair of my Levi's she was wearing. Above the laced-up boot top there was dried blood from a gash in her calf.

"Lillie!" I said. "Why didn't you tell me you were hurt?"

"You couldn't have done anything about it if I had told you, Casey," she answered.

"I'm puttin' you back on your horse and we're trottin' on ahead. . . . And I don't want to hear any argument. It was stupid of you not to tell me, Lillie. Now grab my neck and I'll pick you up and put you on your horse."

"Hey!" Johnnie yelled. *"Damn!* . . . It's the fence! I didn't see it till now, but here she is! I never thought I'd say it, but that's one bobbed-wire fence I'm glad to see!"

"Did you hear that, Casey!" Lillie said. "We've made it! We've made it! All we've got to do now is drive the cows across the fence."

I helped Lillie back into her saddle and then trotted to where Johnnie was busy turning the cows south down the fence—which we had reached *without* crossing Trujillo Creek, which meant we were *at least* two miles north of Trujillo Camp!

"I'd hate like hell to be with a herd you were pointin' to the Judith Basin!" I said to him. "There's no damn tellin' where we'd wind up! Maybe Hong Kong! How in the hell did you let us come so far north?"

"Why don't you bitch a little bit, Casey!" he said.

"I'd have to say I did a pretty goddamn good job of pointin' considering the goddamn circumstances!"

"There's a gate just this side of the creek, about a half mile on down the fence," I said. "We can throw 'em through right there."

"Well hell, thanks for lettin' me know that, Casey," Johnnie said. "I just came in here on a load a punkins and don't know a goddamn thing about punchin' cows!"

"Well . . . dammit, Johnnie," I said, "I think Lillie's leg may be frozen! She's got a bad cut on her leg, and I'm worried about her. *You* tell her we're still over two miles from Trujillo Camp!"

"No need to, Casey!" Lillie yelled right behind me. "You just did! At least we won't have to face the wind anymore." Then she yelled at the cows and trotted down the fence behind them.

"Hell, Casey! That gal's got more balls than you do," Johnnie said. Then he started to laugh. "Damn, I think she's got more balls than me and you and Ab all put together!"

CHAPTER
24

As soon as we came to the gate above Trujillo Creek, we kicked the cows through it. They were in Texas again. They were back on the XIT.

We'd done what we set out to do, and as far as we were concerned Tatum Stagg could go to hell. Or he could go to heaven or Montana or Mexico or anywhere. No matter where he went, our account with him was now settled and closed out.

But we didn't take time to celebrate after turning those cows loose on the XIT. What we did was to strike a long lope south, on the Texas side of the fence, and not pull up until we were at Trujillo Camp.

I carried Lillie through the door while Johnnie and Ab carried a bedroll from the east room into the kitchen and put it in front of the stove for me to lay Lillie on.

Ab stoked the stove with wood and put a pot of coffee on to boil while me and Johnnie helped Lillie out of her blanket and coat and pulled off her boots.

"How do your feet feel?" Johnnie asked.

"They hurt something terrible," Lillie answered.

"Well, that's good," Johnnie said. "Mine do too, but that means they're still alive. Dead things don't hurt."

I pushed Lillie's left Levi's leg and the riding skirt underneath it up to her knee. "Ab," I said, "we're gonna need some water to clean this leg up."

Johnnie looked at the leg and let out a low whistle.

"What does it look like?" Lillie asked, lying back with a grimace on her face.

Ab stepped over to see. "Lord, it looks like . . . terrible!"

Through clenched teeth, Lillie said, "That's a terrible thing to say to a woman about her leg, Ab."

"Oh . . . I didn't mean that, Lillie," Ab said. "Your leg looks good, *real* good. . . . But I don't mean like *that* either! I mean—"

"She knows what you mean, Ab," Johnnie said. "And so do me and Casey." Johnnie looked at me and winked.

"Dang you, Johnnie!" Ab scolded. "I didn't mean that! I didn't mean nothin' disrespectful at all!"

"What about that water?" I asked.

Ab set down a bucket of water on the floor beside the bedroll.

"First, we'll get some of this dried blood soaked off it," I said as I laid a wet rag over the outside of her calf, about two inches below the knee. Just the weight of the rag on the cut made her gasp, stiffen and clench her fists.

I looked at Johnnie. He raised his eyebrows and said, "Ab, why don't you pour a little of that whiskey we been savin' into a cup and give Lillie a swaller of it."

After the rag had been on her leg for two minutes, I soaked it in the water again and said, "I'll be as easy as I can, Lillie, but I've got to get some of this dried blood off so I can see the cut."

"I'm probably just being a big baby," she said as she gasped again.

I started with the dried blood around the cut itself. It seemed to me that Lillie's leg was swelling from her ankle to her knee, which was a strange way for a cut only a few hours old to be acting.

In a couple minutes I had her leg clean except for the cut itself, which was about two inches long up and down her leg. The edges of the cut were swelled apart and filled with dried blood. I used the tip of my knife blade to lift up one end of the blood and then was able to carefully lift it all out at once.

There was something—a narrow, grayish-colored something—in the cut. To find out what it was, I touched it with my knife blade. To my surprise, it was hard, and the instant the blade touched it Lillie yelled and almost went through the roof.

"Dang," I muttered.

"I'm sorry," Lillie said, "it kind of took me by surprise is all."

"It looks like you've got a hunk of rock in your leg, Lillie," I told her.

"What?" Lillie said, as Johnnie and Ab hovered over her leg so they could see. "Maybe that's why it's been hurtin' so much."

"Hurtin'!" Johnnie said. "I imagine it has! You shoulda told somebody, Lillie. That hunk of rock's gotta come outa there before gangrene sets in."

"I'll go get that doc in Tascosa," Ab said.

"In this?" Lillie said, meaning the snowstorm outside.

"She's right," Johnnie said. "Even if a man could keep from gettin' lost, it's over fifty miles each way, and with this weather that could take a day and a half."

"Then you boys will have to get it out," Lillie said, stating the obvious to three cowboys who had performed about every kind of gruesome surgery imaginable on the limbs of horses and cows and each other, but never on a woman!

"I'll boil some more water," Ab said.

I rolled up my sleeves. As much as I didn't look forward to digging the rock out, I didn't really think it would amount to much.

I was wrong. It was more like a knife blade made of rock. It wasn't something that had gotten into Lillie's leg as an afterthought after she had cut it when we both went to the bottom of the trail coming off the mesa in a hell of a tangled mess. It was what had cut her leg to begin with, and it was about an inch wide and an inch deep in the calf of her leg.

By the time I finally got it pulled out, Lillie was no longer conscious. She had bitten down on a rag that Ab gave her, had told Ab and Johnnie to hold her down so she couldn't kick, had broken into a cold sweat and then passed out. While she was unconscious I was able to get every little piece of rock out that I could see, as well as all the grass and dirt. Then we flushed the cut out several times with coal oil and bandaged it with strips of cloth gotten from ripping up Johnnie's extra shirt.

"Can't see how she took it," Ab said. "Ridin' that far with that rock in her leg. And losin' that much blood had to've made her weak."

"And cold," Johnnie said. "My toes were so cold I wanted to cry, and I was plumb full of blood."

"If I had a horse with that kind of heart," Ab said, "I could gather half of Texas by myself." Then Ab lowered his voice as he leaned closer to Johnnie and said, "And you say she's that Raven gal in Tascosa that you—"

"No," Johnnie said quickly, glancing toward me and then looking back down into Lillie's face, "I was wrong about that, Ab. This ain't Raven at all. Ain't even much resemblance 'cept for the black hair. This gal is Lillie Johnson."

Among some people it's the schools you've been to and the fancy way you can talk that's most admired. Some places, it may be the bloat of your wallet that draws the most admiration. But in a cow country people respect things like getting back on top of the horse that you just crawled out from underneath; pulling your end of the load; suffering pain in silence; doing what has to be done and what you see as right.

While we were bandaging Lillie's leg, I remembered something Josh had done one time when he quicked a horse's hoof with a horseshoe nail—he rubbed bacon grease on the nail and threw it in the fire. I laughed at him, but he swore the horse, any horse or any person who had been wounded by an object of any kind, would heal fine if you rubbed bacon grease on the object and then threw it in a fire. So, just to cover as many possible preventions for infection as was medically possible, when we were finished bandaging

Lillie's leg I rubbed bacon grease on the sliver of rock and threw it in the stove.

Although no one can say for sure how much the burning of the rock that came out of Lillie's leg had to do with it, it seemed like her leg *did* begin healing and almost, or so it seemed, as soon as I closed the door on the stove. It had to have been painful for the next few days, but she never complained. And she didn't complain when we washed it out with coal oil twice a day either.

It didn't snow much more after we got to the camp that night. But it stayed cold for the next couple of days, probably around zero judging by the ice on the water troughs at the windmills and the springs that I helped Ab and Johnnie chop holes in so the cattle could drink. I didn't have anything pressing to do, and Lillie couldn't ride yet, so after I rode back to Rana Canyon to get my bedroll and my other horse I lent a hand to Ab and Johnnie. Lillie jumped in and helped out, too, by cooking and keeping house for us.

Just knowing Lillie would be in the house when we got through riding the fence or breaking ice or skinning out dead cattle and knowing she would have the house warm and the coffee on and she would be pretty and smiling when we got there was sure something to look forward to. And it made us all realize, if we didn't already, that this was one of the things a drifter misses the most—a bright smile and a warm fire to come home to . . . a bright smile and a warm fire to turn a shack into a home.

On the morning of the fifth day the sun rose, no longer behind a heavy veil of clouds but in red dawn that quickly gave way to a sky of blue in which not even a single, solitary cloud could be seen lingering anywhere, not even in the farthest corners of the world where one horizon met another.

I shot a young turkey hen that morning at a spring along a little no-name creek a few miles northwest of the camp. I had gone there to chop ice and came upon the flock of turkeys by accident. I was able to get close enough to try a head shot with my Winchester and lucky enough to drop the hen as she was scratching through the snow to the cottonwood leaves along the creek.

When I came trotting into the camp later with the turkey hanging upside down from my saddle horn, I saw Lillie waving at me as she sat on the doorstep of the house enjoying the sunshine. I waved back to her. I didn't see Johnnie's or Ab's horses anywhere and thought they hadn't gotten back yet. I thought I could be alone with Lillie. But as I was opening the gate of the horse corrals, my horse nickered, looking toward the south with his ears perked up. "Dammit," I whispered to myself. Johnnie and Ab were coming.

We had unsaddled the horses and were feeding them when Lillie came to the barn. By then she walked with only a little bit of a limp.

The turkey was hanging on a nail driven into the saddle house wall. She looked at the bird with a big grin.

"Why the grin?" I asked.

"Why the turkey?" she asked in return.

"Just came upon a little bunch of 'em close to a spring. Thought turkey meat might be a change from XIT beef."

"It will be," she said. "And especially since I *think* it's Christmas!"

"Christmas?" Ab and Johnnie said it almost at the same time.

"Why, it sure must be close," I said. "I'd plumb forgot about it, though."

"I had too," Lillie said, "until I saw you coming in with that turkey hanging from your saddle horn. Then it just dawned on me that with what all has happened I'd forgotten all about Christmas—and it may *not* be Christmas exactly. Maybe it was yesterday or maybe it's tomorrow. I've lost track of the days and there's no calendar but—"

"It's close enough for me," Johnnie said.

Lillie took the turkey from the wall. "I'll go start boiling some water so I can pluck it."

I took the turkey from her. "You boil the water and I'll do the pluckin'," I said.

"I'll take some more wood into the house," Johnnie said. "Since it's Christmas and we've already got the ice broke everywhere we need to, I think anything else that needs doin' on this outfit can wait until tomorrow."

That Christmas dinner at Trujillo Camp will be the one I'll remember above all other Christmas dinners.

By the time the meal was ready, the sun, still drifting in a cloudless sky, was no more than two hours above the western horizon and the shadows were lengthening. The water that had been dripping off the house and the barn had gotten too stiff to drip any longer.

There were only two chairs in the house, but Ab and Johnnie rolled their bedrolls and sat on them.

The meal itself was simple—roast turkey, gravy from canned milk, beans, fresh bread and hot coffee.

"Christmas, eighteen eighty-seven," Johnnie said as he sat on his bedroll and grabbed a knife in one hand and a fork in the other. He'd started to stab a slice of roast turkey when Ab elbowed him and gestured toward Lillie with his head. Lillie was sitting with her head bowed. Slowly us three cowboys laid our knives and forks down and bowed our heads.

"Thank you, God," she whispered, "for food . . ." Then there was a long silence, except for a pair of coyotes howling and barking south of the house. I wondered if Lillie was through and if she was why didn't she say Amen. I glanced up at Johnnie, and he was glancing at Ab. Ab shrugged his shoulders. Then Lillie, with breaking voice, said, ". . . and for friends. Amen."

While we were eating Lillie said, "I want all of you to know that this is the nicest Christmas I have ever known. I want to thank you for letting me share it with you."

"Shoot," Johnnie said with a smile, "this ain't nothin' special. All of this"—he waved his hand around the room—"or something ever' bit as fancy could be yours forever if you'd just take old Casey up on his proposal."

"And then as soon as you get married," Ab said in a sudden burst of wordiness, "you can adopt me an' Johnnie."

We all laughed, but as I laughed I kept glancing at Lillie to see if I could tell what she was really thinking.

When the laughter faded away, Lillie reached for the turkey and said, "I'm afraid Casey withdrew his offer, boys. Said he wouldn't have me on a bet."

"After she turned me down," I said. "She said out of all the things she had done in her life that she regretted, missing out on the chance to be Mrs. Casey Wills was not one of them."

Lillie smiled. "He said"—she began counting on her fingers—"that he was never serious about marrying me; that he was a big-outfit cowboy; that he was *not* a, let me see, that he was *not* a mare-riding, square-bread-eating nester of a homesteader with plow dirt under his fingernails who would let some woman lead him around by the nose."

Ab and Johnnie whooped and hollered.

After we'd eaten all we could hold and had drunk a pot of coffee, Johnnie brought out the bottle of whiskey he and Ab had in the house and said, "There's just enough in here for one Christmas toast," and then he poured a little in each of our empty coffee cups, letting the last few drops drip directly from the bottle onto his tongue.

We all stood up. "Who'll make a toast?" Johnnie asked.

"We each will," Lillie said. "We don't have enough liquor for a drink after each toast, so we'll each make a toast and then we'll have our drink. You first, Johnnie."

Johnnie quickly raised his cup and without hesitation said, "To bad horses and good women . . . or whichever way you like 'em."

We all laughed, but I thought I saw a blush on Lillie's face. "Ab?" she said.

Ab raised his cup. His face was strangely solemn. "To Mama and Papa and home and to Christmas with them . . . next year."

That made us all a little solemn, quietened us down some.

Lillie looked at me with her big, dark eyes. "Casey?"

I lifted my cup and looked at it. I didn't look at nothing else. "Here's to Josh," I said. "Who's safely across the Missouri at last."

A stillness came over the room. A loneliness. An awful truth.

Then it was Lillie's turn, but for a while I didn't know if she was ever going to say anything. But then she did—"Here's to Ab and Johnnie, how I love them. . . . And here's to Casey, the only man who has ever touched me. . . . And here's to our sins, may we always remember how easy they are committed and how hard forgotten."

Then Lillie held her cup out, and we all touched our cups to hers and to each other's. Then we had our drink and sat back down.

"Seems like we oughta sing a Christmas song," Johnnie said.

"Say that poem you know about Christmas," Ab said to Johnnie.

Johnnie scratched his head and scooted his bedroll back. "Well, all right. Here goes," he said. "The wages that a cowboy earns in summer go like smoke, and when winter snows have come you can bet your life he's broke. My saddle and my gun's in soak and my spurs I've long since sold; my rawhide and quirt are gone; my chaps!—no, they're too dang old. Yeah, my stuff's all gone, I can't even beg a smoke, for no one cares about a puncher who is broke." Johnnie bowed and sat down and we clapped.

"That's really good," Lillie said, "but what does it have to do with Christmas?"

"Danged if I know," Johnnie said, "but the feller who taught it to me said it was about Christmas, so I figure it must be."

Just as we started to laugh, the door was pushed open—by none other than George Findlay, the friendly Chicago bookkeeper!

"Well! Hello, Mr. Findlay!" Johnnie said. "Don't guess we even heard you ride up. Come on in."

Findlay stepped inside and closed the door behind him. He took off his fogged-up wire-rim glasses and cleaned them with a handkerchief he pulled out of a coat pocket.

"How 'bout somethin' to eat?" Johnnie said. "Ain't much left, but you're welcome to it. Got plenty of coffee, though. Gettin' cold out there again, ain't it? Here, set down on this bedroll."

"Keep your seat, Mr. Lester," Findlay said. "I won't be here long. I've got to meet a wagon in Endee, but I thought I'd come by and see how you and Ab were getting by. It looks like you're certainly enjoying yourselves."

"Sure are," Johnnie said. "You know Casey Wills, I think—and this lady is Miss Lillie Johnson."

Findlay put his glasses back on and looked at me and Lillie. Then he said, stiff as a poker, "I should know him—I fired him not long ago. I don't know the . . . the lady, but I think I know of her. We have rules, Mr. Lester. . . . Where is the list of rules I gave you? It's supposed to be posted in plain sight."

"Oh, it's in plain sight," Johnnie said. "That list of rules is hangin' out in the privy. Leastways it was. . . . Ab, did we use that paper that had all the rules listed on it?"

"Not yet," Ab said.

"See?" Johnnie said with an innocent shrug.

"What are these people doing here?" Findlay asked.

"We've been celebratin' Christmas," Johnnie said. I could tell he was getting hot. "Casey shot a young turkey hen, and Lillie cooked it for us."

"Christmas was two days ago." You could figure a bookkeeper would know exactly when Christmas was.

"It was today here at Trujillo Camp," Johnnie said.

"I think you know very well there is a rule against having any intoxicating drinks of any kind on company property, don't you, Mr. Lester?"

"Well, now you see, Mr. Findlay," Johnnie said, making a big gesture with his hands as he spoke, "that there bottle on the table is empty. It's just there for decorational purposes . . . And! . . . And, I emptied it *across* the fence, over in the Territory of New Mexico."

"Shall I state rule number three for you, Mr. Lester?" Now Findlay was getting hot. "Nobody whose employment has been terminated by the company shall be allowed to remain in any camp."

"The only rule that's ever meant anything on any outfit I ever worked for, Mr. Findlay," Johnnie said rather calmly, "is that you take care of the outfit's cattle like they were your own."

"Rule six—"

"Oh sit down, Findlay," Johnnie said with a smile that I knew was not exactly a good-natured smile, "and have some beans and bread. You don't have to eat none of this old sinful turkey, but I'm tired of hearin' you spout off about rules—rules that were drawed up by a bunch of stiff-necked pencil pushers who couldn't gather a milk-pen calf out of the water lot. Hell, Casey and Lillie here have been helpin' me an' Ab for several days."

"You get them off XIT land before dark, and I'll forget about all the rule infractions, *this* time."

"Get them off? What are you talkin' about, Findlay?"

"Loafers, deadbeats, tramps, gamblers or disreputable persons must not be entertained at any camp, nor will—"

I never seen Johnnie or Ab either one move any faster. Before Findlay knew what had happened, they each had an arm and had him pinned against the door with his feet three inches off the floor.

"Rule number one, Mr. Findlay," Ab growled, "you don't insult our friends."

"And rule number two," Johnnie whispered, "you sure as thunder don't insult our lady friends!"

"Rule number three"—Ab again—"and when you do, you apologize!"

"I . . . I actually *didn't* mean to insult anybody."

"Tell *her!*" Johnnie said, pressing him harder against the door.

"I'm . . . sorry, ma'am. I didn't mean any disrespect to you."

They let Findlay down slowly until he was again standing on the floor. He straightened his glasses and he straightened his coat and he said, "You know what this means, of course?"

"Yeah," Johnnie said, "it means we quit this Chicago-minded, nester-run outfit, and as bad as you'd like to talk us out of it, you ain't even gonna try, are you?"

"I'm certainly not," Findlay muttered. "The usual procedure is for me to give you and Mr. Deacons pay vouchers that you would take to Alamocitas. But under the circumstances, when I get to Endee I'll instruct Mr. Franks to pay you in cash and I'll send him a check. I'll expect you to be out of here by dark tomorrow . . . *all* of you."

"Don't let the door hit you in the butt on your way out, Mr. Findlay," Johnnie said.

When Findlay was gone, Lillie said softly, "I'm so sorry. I feel like if I hadn't been here—"

"Gal," Johnnie said, "you've got to learn to quit apologizin' for things that aren't any of your doing." Then he looked at Ab and said, "Besides, we was ready to roll our beds anyway, wasn't we, Ab? This honest work ain't what folks try to make it out to be anyway. Shoot, if we'd a stayed we mighta even wound up doin' what Casey and Josh did—greasin' windmills! Then we'd probably get to where we couldn't sleep at night for worryin' what rules we'd broke that day."

"I've been fired from better outfits than this," Ab said.

"We didn't get fired, Ab," Johnnie reminded him. "We quit. It's just a shame we don't have any more whiskey so we could get drunk and celebrate our good fortune and our good sense."

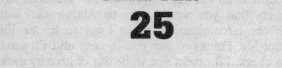

By quick democratic process we decided not to leave after sundown but to spend the night at Trujillo Camp and leave the next morning. As was always the arrangement, Lillie slept in the kitchen beside the fire while us three cowboys slept in the east room. That night, though, our last at Trujillo Camp, I couldn't sleep, so after I was sure Johnnie and Ab were asleep I tiptoed into the kitchen.

"Is that you, Casey?" Lillie whispered as I slowly pushed the kitchen door open.

"Yeah," I whispered as I stepped into the kitchen and partly closed the door between the rooms, "it's me. Thought we might talk a spell."

I stepped toward the stove and sat down at the foot of Lillie's bedroll. We kept our voices low. "What're you going to do now? Go back east? Go home?"

"I can't go home, Casey," she said. "What are *you* going to do?"

"Oh . . . I don't know," I answered honestly. "Me

and Ab and Johnnie will go somewhere and hire on to some cow outfit."

"But where?"

I sort of laughed. "Who knows? Maybe the wind and God know, but they haven't told me yet. Could be south Texas or Arizona for now; then maybe we can get on with a trail outfit headin' north in the spring. There's a lot of breedin' cattle going to Montana."

"I'll go with you!" Lillie blurted out. Her saying that took me by such surprise that my tongue couldn't do anything but lie on the floor of my mouth like a piece of raw beef. Then she said, kind of embarrassed, "That is, if you want me to, Casey."

I still couldn't say anything. All I could do was to just sit there in the nearly total darkness and listen to the cedar wood pop in the stove. Finally, after what seemed like a long time, I said, "Yeah, I want you to, Lillie—I want you to real bad. . . . But it wouldn't be any good, not for you, anyway. Not following some drifter like me around."

"What . . . what do you mean, Casey? I thought—"

"I mean," I said, "that lots of times I'd be sleepin' out with some chuck wagon for weeks at a time, and you couldn't go. Outfits don't allow women with the wagon, leastways I never heard of one that did."

"Then I could get a job in the nearest town and wait for you, Casey. Maybe you could come in sometimes on the weekends and—"

"And how long are you going to wait and in how many towns, Lillie?" I asked her.

"Maybe, after a while we'd find a place we liked so much we would want to stay and—"

"And I could get a job in a hardware store? Or

maybe clean out the livery and sweep the saloon floor at night?"

"Well, I don't know." Her voice was softer. "I thought maybe you could—"

"Could *what*, Lillie? I'm a cowboy. It's what I do. It's all I know how to do."

"You really just don't want me to go with you, do you, Casey?" Her voice was beginning to quiver. "Is it because of what I was?"

I turned to her, and although I could barely see her in the dark room, I stroked her thick, soft hair. "Don't want you to go with me?" I said. "Every bit of my body, every ounce of my heart wants you to go with me, Lillie. I've wanted it since the day I first saw you—the day I borrowed two cents from you for postage. Yes! I want you with me, and when you're not with me I want you waiting for me. When I crawl in my bedroll at night, night after night, week after week, I want to know that you're waiting for me, that you can't think of nothin' else except the day I'll come ridin' in.

"But it wouldn't be any kind of life for you. We'd have a night, or maybe two or three, and then I'd ride out again and tell you I'd meet you in Socorro in six weeks, or Lander in seven weeks, and if I'm not there in seven weeks I'll be there in eight for sure."

Suddenly she was in my arms, and I was kissing her neck, smelling her hair and feeling it soft against my face. In the dark I hadn't noticed that she'd taken off her clothes and was sleeping in one of my old shirts. But now I knew it.

"I *will* wait for you, Casey," she whispered as I kissed her chin, then—as my lips found hers—"I will."

I knew she hadn't taken what I'd said the way I'd meant it, but it didn't matter, not with me tasting the sweetness of her kiss and feeling the fullness of her breasts against my body. Nothing mattered then, not having her follow me from one jerkwater town to another, me not having any real future to promise her, not what would happen if she got pregnant, not what she'd said a few days ago on the mesa above Tatum Stagg's ranch—"The more I'm with you the less difference I can see between you and Tatum." *Nothing* mattered but how she smelled and tasted and how soft and warm her breasts were—even through the two layers of cotton fabric separating us.

I fumbled at the top button on her shirt—fumbled and fumbled while we kissed but still couldn't get it pushed back through the buttonhole. Finally the button slid through the hole and my hand slid inside the shirt and my fingers touched . . . gently touched and caressed flesh as soft and velvety as only a woman's flesh can be.

But suddenly Lillie was trembling. "I . . . I'm afraid, Casey," she whispered. "I've made so many mistakes. . . . But I know I can trust you. I know you're not like other men, and you're sure nothing like Tatum. You have honor and integrity and—"

"Hey, Casey!" It was Johnnie yelling from the other room.

Lillie and I jerked apart, and I stood up. Lillie held on to my hand in the dark for a few seconds, and then she let it go. "See you in the morning," she whispered.

I opened and shut the outside door just loud enough so I thought Johnnie should be able to hear it, and then I opened the door between the rooms, stepped into the dim lantern light and said, like I didn't want to wake Lillie, "I was outside takin' a leak. What're you hollerin' about?"

"Can't sleep," Johnnie said as he rolled a cigarette. "When did you start goin' out in the snow in your bare feet to take a leak?"

"Been doin' it a long time," I said. "It's none of your business if I go out to take a leak naked."

"Hell. . . . You were talkin' to Lillie."

"That's none of your business either."

"What's she going to do?" he asked.

"I guess she's goin' with us."

"Goin' where with us?"

I shrugged. "Wherever we go, I guess. She'll wait in the closest town to whatever outfit we're workin' for."

"You got it bad, don't you, Casey? Well, hell, why don't you just get married and get it over with? You ain't never going to be any count anymore anyway."

"Blow out the lantern and shut up, Johnnie," I said. "I don't feel like arguin' with you."

Johnnie blew out the lantern all right, but he wasn't quite ready to shut up. "You and Lillie *ought* to get married," he said in the dark, "and raise a bunch of kids. In Kansas, where there's fertile soil and lots of farms and farmers, real stable kind of folks, churchgoing, settled folks. Kansas is a good place to be married and raise kids in."

"What in the hell would you know about that?" I asked.

"I guess I know as much about it as you do," Johnnie said.

"Well, I never said a damn word about Kansas."

Johnnie laughed. "No, I guess you never did, but it's a damn good place to farm and raise kids anyway."

"And this was a good place to sleep a few minutes ago," Ab growled.

"Well, don't blame me, Ab," Johnnie said. "Old Casey here and Lillie woke me up makin' plans to go to Kansas and raise snotty-nosed kids."

Ab sat up in his bedroll. "Kansas?" he said. "Casey, are you—"

I pulled the blankets in my bedroll up over my shoulder. "Forget it, Ab," I said. "Nobody's going to Kansas. Johnnie's got gas from those Christmas beans we ate."

Johnnie giggled but didn't say any more. In a few minutes I could hear him and Ab both snoring again. But I didn't snore. I couldn't keep from thinking about Lillie. I thought about kissing her and touching her velvety flesh and how she felt in my arms of course. I thought a lot about what she'd said about me having honor and integrity. When you've convinced yourself that you have those qualities, it creates a feeling that fits pretty good and feels mighty comfortable. But when somebody you care about a lot is convinced you have them, suddenly you're not so sure anymore, and that comfortable feeling becomes a pretty heavy burden to bear.

We didn't leave Trujillo Camp at first light the next morning, because one of Johnnie's horses was about to lose a shoe. Johnnie reset the shoes all the way around on the horse while me and Ab drank coffee and watched him. The sun was bright, and water had started dripping off the saddle house roof by the time we were ready to leave.

"There's something about ridin' away from an outfit like this that makes a man feel good inside," Johnnie said as we rode through the gate just west of the house.

He was right, too. It felt damn good to be shed of the XIT. Felt like spring after a bad winter. Felt like a bath and clean clothes when you hadn't had either for days. Felt like clean sheets. Felt free.

"Hear you're goin' with us," Johnnie twisted in his saddle and said to Lillie.

"I'm going with *Casey*," she said firmly but with a smile.

CHAPTER
26

The late-morning sun was so bright reflecting off the melting snow that it was impossible not to squint as we rode to Endee. We weren't going to be there long. Lillie had to get her things—at least as much as she could pack into two bags. Two bags was the most I thought we could tie onto the bay horse along with my bedroll. And, of course, Johnnie and Ab had to pick up the XIT money that George Findlay was to have left there with Lloyd Franks.

There were no horses tied to the hitching rail in front of the lone building in Endee, which meant, more than likely, that Tatum Stagg and his men were not there. We wouldn't have *not* gone in if they had been, but anybody with any common sense at all could see we had nothing to gain by being in the same town as Stagg and his bunch—especially if that town had only one street and one building.

Johnnie and Ab got their money—ten dollars each

221

—while Lillie went upstairs to room 212 to pack her bags.

While we were waiting for Lillie to come back downstairs, Johnnie said to Lloyd Franks, "Mr. Franks, we've been on the trail for a mighty long spell, and I do believe it was about the dustiest goddamn trail I've ever had the misfortune to travel over."

Franks looked at Johnnie with one eye cocked and said, "What're you talkin' about? Didn't y'all just come from Trujillo Camp?"

"Sure enough," Johnnie answered.

"But that ain't but twelve miles—and the ground's covered with snow," Franks said.

"Yeah, well . . . there was plenty of dust underneath that snow, believe me. Therefore, drinks are in order, Mr. Franks, for me and my friends. . . . I guess old George Findlay told you to give us a bottle and put it on the XIT account, didn't he? Like he told us he was going to?"

Franks smiled. "Hardly," he said.

So Johnnie bought us all a drink, and after we'd had that drink he laid some more money on the bar top and bought us all another. While Franks was pouring the second drink, Johnnie laid more money out and told him to just leave the bottle. When Johnnie had money, his friends had money. Or rather, when Johnnie had money he had whiskey and his friends had whiskey, too.

"Reckon you might need that money, Johnnie?" I said. "We're plumb outa honest work, you know, and it's a long time till spring. If we don't—"

"Quit worryin', Casey," he said. "I know you've still got that money Stagg gave you and Josh."

"It don't seem right, though," I said.

"Well, I think it's the least Stagg owes us for takin' all those stray cattle. But if you *really* don't feel right about keeping it, then you can let me carry it."

"I'll carry it," I said.

Johnnie looked toward the stairs, pointed to them with a thumb and said, "What're you going to do with her?"

"What do you mean 'What am I goin' to do with her?' You talk like she's a cow."

"Well, Casey," Ab said, "he just means . . ." Ab thought for a few seconds and then said, "He just means . . . Well, you know—what're you going to do with her now?"

"Thanks for clearin' that up, Ab," Johnnie said.

"I'm not doing anything with her," I said. "She can do whatever she wants, but I think she wants to go with us."

"Like she had any other choice," Johnnie said.

"Yeah," Ab threw in, "she can either go with us or stay here with Stagg."

"Who was that old boy that had that redhead followin' him around for so long?" Ab asked.

"Dominick Dick O'Grady," I answered.

"Also known as Dominecker Pecker," Johnnie said. "I heard old Red drank herself to death in a hotel room in Chadron, Nebraska, waitin' for old Dominick to come through with a trail herd."

"It ain't gonna be that way," I said.

"Well, I never thought it was," Johnnie shot back.

"Just make sure you don't," I warned.

There was a small commotion out on the porch, ending with a man growling, "I'll box both your ears if you don't stop!"

Then the door opened and a tall, stooped man with

long arms and legs and wearing a dirty, floppy hat stepped through. He was followed by four dirty kids in tattered clothing, who were followed by a thin, frail, stringy-haired woman with dark circles under her eyes who was constantly wringing and rubbing her hands.

The troupe stopped just inside the door, and the man, eyeing Lloyd Franks behind the bar, said to him, "We starved out on our homestead and are tryin' to git back to Illinois. The missus or the kids ain't had no food in two days, and I was wonderin' if you had some work I could do. I don't need no cash money, just a little food. If it was just me . . . but it ain't."

The kids all huddled around their mother, wiping their runny noses with shirtsleeves and looking like little scared rabbits. I could see the fear in the mother's eyes too, and the humiliation in the man's. It was easy to see life had been a disappointment for them, a bitter disappointment.

"Sorry, mister," Franks said. "But there ain't no work here."

"Mr. Franks," I said quickly, "has Lillie told you she's leavin'?"

Franks shot me a quick, hard glance and said, "She's told me, but my missus can handle the job this winter. Business is slow anyway."

I looked down at the table we were sitting around so as not to have to see the pitiful sight the family offered or their desperation.

The man said a heartbroken "Thank you, we'll make out." And that's when I glanced back up at them and saw, for just an instant, not the man and woman who were really there but me and Lillie! I batted my eyes and, much to my relief, the other man and woman came back to their sniffly-nosed tribe. Must of been the whiskey, I thought.

As they turned to leave I suddenly heard myself saying to them, "Did you start out thinkin' you could make it work?"

The family all looked at me for a few seconds with blank stares and then started on out the door. Johnnie and Ab looked at me with blank stares, too, and then Johnnie reached over and slid the whiskey out of my reach.

"Wait!" I said as the man was closing the door. "Give 'em a sack of food, Mr. Franks. Give 'em *two* sacks, and I'll pay for it."

"You sure you can?" Franks asked.

"Yeah," I said, pulling out the roll of money Stagg had left for me and Josh and letting Franks see it.

The man with the hungry kids and wife stood just inside the door. It was hard to tell what he was thinking, but I figured he was thinking he didn't want charity, but there was the wife and kids.

"Take it," Johnnie said to the man standing at the door. "He's a rich man. Runs a lot of cattle."

"Yeah," Ab said. "Runs 'em outa the brush and off the rimrocks . . . and sometimes he runs bobcats, too."

Johnnie and Ab saw more than a little humor in that.

After Franks had given the two sacks of food to the man at the door, and the man at the door had tipped his hat and said thanks and disappeared, Franks came to our table to collect. "It came to two six bits," he said.

As I was paying Franks, Johnnie said, "We'd better

get him out of here, Ab, before he spends our whole damn inheritance."

Ab said, "Yeah, but let's eat first. Mr. Franks, set us all up to a big feed. Lillie'll be eatin' with us too. Don't hold nothin' good back. I'll pay. We're going to leave Endee with a full belly anyway."

"Do you know why these joints serve whiskey?" I asked.

"Let's see," Johnnie said. "Is it because it promotes health and contributes to the brotherhood of men?"

"No," I answered. "It's because once a man gets past his second drink he suddenly feels rich and forgets how poor he really is. Take you two, for instance—in the middle of winter with no job, no idea where you're goin' or how you're goin' to live till spring, and here you are buyin' whiskey and orderin' big feeds instead of drinkin' water and eatin' latigo soup."

"But me and Ab both have got a rich friend!" Johnnie said, pouring us all another drink. "Hell, he's got money to give to strangers even."

"Well," I said with a grin, "too bad you're not strangers, ain't it?"

Mary Franks came in to help her husband put the feed bag on for us. As she was wiping a glass behind the counter, she looked at me, not too congenial, and said, "I understand Lillie's going with you. You be good to her, you hear?"

"Yes, ma'am," I said, with more doubt in my voice than I wanted to show.

Lillie came downstairs about the time the food was being carried to our table. She had fixed her hair up on top of her head and had put on clean riding clothes. She looked beautiful, so beautiful about all I could do was to look at her and pull her chair out for her. She looked like a proper lady. She looked like she should have been somebody's wife, living in a nice house with a white picket fence around it.

"Let's eat," I heard Ab say at the same time I heard the door open behind me and saw the smile and color suddenly drain from Lillie's face, saw her dark eyes grow big with fear, heard her utter a short gasp.

"Uh-oh at the front door," Ab said as he lifted a biscuit to his mouth.

"Stagg?" I said under my breath.

"Uh-huh," Ab said.

"He look mad?" I asked, which was a dumb question.

"As an old wet hen," Ab said.

"Just keep eatin' and ignore him," I said.

"What about that double-barreled ten gauge?" Ab asked as he cut himself off a bite of beef. "You want me to ignore that too?"

"Sure," Johnnie answered. Then he said loudly, "Really good eatin', ain't it? Hand me another biscuit." He whispered, "Keep both hands on top of the table, Casey. . . . I'm puttin' my Colt in your lap, butt to the right."

CHAPTER
27

As Stagg walked across the hotel floor, he came into my vision. My eyes followed him then all the way to the bar while my right hand slid off the table, into my lap and around the butt of Johnnie's Colt.

I was nervous, scared even. I'd never shot at a man before and was hoping I'd be able to say the same thing after the next few minutes had passed. I had no use for Tatum Stagg, but I had no desire to kill him either, in spite of what he'd done to me and Josh and Lillie. I figured my account with him was closed when we shut the gate behind those thirty-two head of XIT cows. The trouble was, I had a hunch that Stagg and I used different accounting methods and he still wanted to square things with me.

When Stagg got to the bar, he turned around to face our table. There was only about twenty feet separating us now. His shotgun was cradled in his right arm, and my right thumb was nervously rubbing the hammer of Johnnie's Colt. Shotguns and nervous hammer thumbs are always a dangerous combination.

"Goddamn you, Wills," he said again, just like he'd said when he caught me with the XIT cows the first time I tried to take them back. He said it low and mean, the muscles in his jaws twitching. "You never shoulda crossed me. Why didn't you take me up on my offer in the first place? What's the XIT ever done for you?"

"Gave me an honest wage for honest work," I said.

"And then fired you," Stagg said. "Why did you take those goddamn cows back for 'em?"

"Didn't do it for *them*—did it for me and Josh . . . and Lillie."

Stagg's eyes got even smaller and colder. "And Lillie," he said. "What're you thinkin' of, Lillie? What're you doin'!"

"I'm . . . I'm going with Casey, Tatum," she said.

Stagg laughed, not loud but low. "You're not goin' anywhere I don't tell you to. Now get up and get me a drink."

"No!" she replied.

Suddenly the muzzle of Stagg's shotgun flew upward and leveled on the table. My hand tightened around the butt of the Colt, but I kept it in my lap, partly because I was still hoping killing could be avoided and partly because Johnnie was directly between me and Stagg.

"If I see any of you men move an inch," Stagg said, thumbing back both hammers of the ten gauge, "I'll open up on the table with both barrels. . . . Now do what I said, Lillie—get me a goddamn drink!"

"Don't hurt anyone," Lillie said. "I'll do it. . . . It's okay, Casey."

Lillie walked slowly behind the bar, poured a shot of whiskey into a shot glass and slid it toward Stagg.

"Bring it to me," he said without taking his eyes or his shotgun off the table. "Bring it around to this side of the bar—on my left. . . . Come on, bring it to me!"

Lillie carried the drink to the public side of the bar and set it on the bar six feet from Stagg.

"I said to bring it *to me,* Lillie," he said. "And stand here at the bar beside me—like you did at the Exchange Saloon in Tascosa when I first saw you."

"Tatum . . . please," Lillie pleaded as she slid reluctantly down the bar until she was standing beside him.

Stagg moved his left hand from the shotgun and used it to touch Lillie's black hair. "Now what're you thinkin', sweetheart?" he said. "You know you can't make it without me. You know that if it wasn't for me you'd still be Raven in Tascosa. . . . You owe me, Lillie. Now come here and give me a hug and we'll forget *all* of this. I'll let these cowboys go and we can go upstairs." Then he pulled her into his left side and put his arm around her.

But Lillie sobbed and struggled to get away from the grasp of his arm. I suddenly thought of the strange dream I'd had about the black spider on Lillie's neck and how she struggled to get away from it.

Suddenly, among struggling and sobbing and a flailing of arms, Lillie's teeth sank into the back of Stagg's broad hand. He swore and let her go.

When she stepped back, she had his .45 in her hands. She was crying uncontrollably and shaking like dried leaves in a high wind, but she held the gun at arm's length with both hands, and she pulled the big hammer to full cock.

Stagg roared in laughter. "Not this again, Lillie!" he shouted. "I would have thought you learned your lesson the last time, when I shot your horse out from underneath you! . . . Now give me the gun."

"Th . . . This time'll be di . . . different, Tatum," she said. "This time I'll kill you . . . if you don't put that shotgun down and get out of here."

Stagg roared in laughter again. "No, Lillie," he said, *"I'm* gonna kill a couple of these cowboys here if you don't put that thing down by the time I count to five."

"I'm warning you, Tatum!" Lillie screamed.

"One. . . . Two. . . . Put it down, Lillie. . . . Three."

I saw Lillie extend her arms even farther, and I saw Stagg's grip tighten on the shotgun.

I had a feeling somebody was going to die in Endee in the next few seconds—but I didn't know who and I didn't know how many.

"Four. . . . *Goddammit, Lillie, I'll kill 'em all!"*

"Tatum! No!" Lillie screamed.

"Fi . . ."

The gun in Lillie's hand roared.

Stagg flinched, and I saw his face grimace in pain.

Johnnie and Ab dove to the floor as I fired toward Stagg without standing up, fired through the tabletop, not knowing whether or not I'd hit him.

Stagg whirled his shotgun toward Lillie as I turned the table over and brought Johnnie's Colt up.

I thumbed the hammer back and fired again, an instant before the ten gauge boomed. Lillie screamed and fell, a window behind her shattered.

Stagg stumbled back against the bar, trying to point his shotgun at Lillie again.

"Don't, Stagg!" I yelled.

But the shotgun's muzzle kept moving toward Lillie.

I thumbed the hammer of the Colt in my hand back and fired again, hitting Stagg in the center of the chest with a .45 caliber slug and slamming him back hard against the bar.

The ten gauge roared again, the blast going into the floor.

Stagg looked at me, then he looked at Lillie lying on the floor. "Goddammit," he said. And then he died on his feet.

I rushed to Lillie. She was unscratched.

"Tatum?" she said. "Is he . . ."

"He's dead, Lillie," I said.

"Did I . . ."

"No," I said. I added, fibbing a little, "You never hit him." I figured, come my own judgment day, that one little white lie wasn't going to make much difference one way or the other, and I figured Lillie had had enough to contend with in her life without having to deal with the fact that she shot Tatum Stagg. I was going to have a tough enough time dealing with it myself—and I was a big old tough cowboy.

That was the first time I'd killed a man outright, and, although I knew I had had no other choice and felt no remorse, I also felt it was not something a man should take any particular pride in.

Maybe I shouldn't have been so damn insistent on seeing that those thirty-three head of cows got back to the XIT, but I never saw it that way. A man does what he has to do in order to be able to live with himself—in a nutshell, that's really all I know about life.

We didn't leave Endee that day like we had planned because Lillie wasn't in any condition to leave for several hours after the killing of Tatum Stagg. She was getting herself together about as fast as any woman could have under the circumstances though, and by sundown I think she could have traveled. But we decided to wait until the next day. Lloyd Franks said that, under the circumstances, he would donate a bed to Lillie without charging any rent. He never mentioned anything about any bed donations for me and Ab and Johnnie, so we spooled out our bedrolls on the front porch.

I lay in my bedroll for a long time trying to go to sleep that night, but too much had happened for me to even start to be able to sleep. I wanted to go up and talk to Lillie, as I figured we had a lot of talking we needed to do, but I also figured she needed to rest and wouldn't be in much mood for male company any time real soon.

So I lay in my bedroll and tossed and tumbled and thought about Lillie and the future. Whenever I was able to fall off to sleep, I heard gunfire and saw Tatum Stagg dying over and over.

At the first sign of daylight along the eastern horizon, I smelled coffee, so I slipped on my boots, rolled my bed and went inside.

Lloyd Franks and I didn't have a lot in common to talk about other than the killing of Tatum Stagg, which he wanted to talk about but I didn't.

"When word gets out about this," he said, "people'll be comin' in here and askin' if this is where Tatum Stagg was killed."

"When is the next stage due to come through here?" I asked.

"Due in today as a matter of fact," he said. And then he took out his pocket watch, looked at it and said, "In about six hours—at eleven o'clock—if it's anywheres near to being on schedule. . . . Doubt anybody on that stage will have heard about the killin' yet though."

"We can only hope," I said. "Thanks for the coffee. When Johnnie and Ab wake up, tell 'em I'll be back in a little while."

CHAPTER
28

I saddled my gray and rode south for a couple of miles until I found a trail that led to the top of the caprock. When I topped out, I got off the gray and stood there at the edge of the caprock looking north.

On top of the caprock where I was standing, the sun was already up, but below me the sun was just beginning to rise, and only the tops of the hills and ridges were being touched by the light.

Lord, a man could see a big scope of country from up there. He could see clear across forever and to the edge of eternity. If Endee seemed small and in the middle of nowhere when a man was in it, that was nothing compared to how small and in the middle of nowhere it looked from on top of the caprock. It was hard to believe people lived there—and died there.

It was cold up on top of the caprock. Cold and still and quiet—a good place for a man to think about life and death and all that comes between.

Although death, sooner or later, would surely come

for me, it was life that was at hand now, and life that had to be dealt with now.

So what did I want out of life? A home? A wife and family and all the responsibility that goes with them? Something and someone to hang on to? A sense of belonging—belonging in a certain place and to a certain someone? Yes, I wanted all of those things—and I could have them with Lillie. She and I could make it work.

But . . . God! I drew in a deep breath of cold, clean air and looked down upon the great expanse of . . . of bear grass and cactus and hills and creeks and an ocean of grass and . . . and emptiness and loneliness.

I stood there on the caprock in silence, awed by the scene before me—a scene the likes of which I had looked at thousands of times before—until a chill crept up my spine and slid down it again, a chill brought on not by the cold morning air but by seeing something so breathtaking and wonderfully made it seemed impossible that it even existed.

I wanted a home and all that goes with it, but I wanted *that,* too! All of it—even the emptiness and the loneliness, things as addicting to some men as cheap whiskey is to others.

There was a battle waging somewhere within my head, or my heart, or wherever such battles are waged.

Whoever said a man is a king in his own home may have known what he was talking about, but a drifting cowboy is king of all he surveys, king of the Big Lonely! He owns the sun and the stars, the wind and the rain, the air he breathes and the earth that will someday cover his lonely, forgotten grave.

The battle was finished. The survivor, bruised but

wiser, stepped astraddle of the gray and struck the downward trail toward Endee.

When I got back to Endee, Johnnie and Ab had their horses saddled, and they both had their beds strapped onto their other horses. I didn't stop to talk to them; I went upstairs to talk to Lillie.

"Are you okay, Lillie?" I asked, standing just inside her door with my hat in my hand.

"I think so," she answered. "My ears are still ringing, and God only knows how long it will be before I can close my eyes without seeing the expression on Tatum's face right before he died."

It got quiet in the little room then, and it was a nervous sort of quiet. Something unspoken was being said.

Then, at the same time, we both said, "I've been thinking . . ." We both laughed, but, like the quiet, it was a nervous laugh.

"Okay," Lillie said with a smile, "you go first."

"No. . . . Ladies first," I said.

"No. . . . *You* go first," she said. "What is it you've been thinking, Casey? . . . Have you been thinking that you really *can* do something besides be a cowboy? Have you been thinking about how you're getting tired of drifting from one ranch to another and that you're ready, *really* ready to settle down and buy a house on a corner lot in town with a white picket fence around it and come home to that same house and to the same woman and kids every day for the rest of your life? Have you been thinking that you're ready to trade big roundups and wild cattle for church socials and diapers?"

I rubbed at the floor with the toe of my boot and smiled a little bit. "I don't reckon," I said.

It got quiet again for a few seconds, and then I said, "What happened to the part where you follow me around from one jerkwater town to the next and wait for me to come see you every few weeks?"

"You mean the part where you give up nothing and get everything?" Lillie asked, raising her eyebrows.

"Yeah," I said. "That's it."

That made Lillie laugh one of her really pretty laughs, and then she said, "But that was when you were whispering my name and kissing me on the neck, Casey. At that moment I would have agreed to nearly anything."

My eyes lit up.

"I said *nearly* anything, Casey. . . . But I can't settle for a little kissing and whispering every few weeks. And I can't follow you around from one town to another and sleep with you in a hotel room whenever you can come in and not be giving my integrity away. No—I can't settle for only a little part of you, Casey. I want *all* of you. I want to be your wife. . . . Casey? Casey, I just proposed to you. What do you say?"

I took in a deep breath and let it out slow. "Lillie. . . . Right after we first met, right after that first kiss on the porch, I would have married you in a minute. I wanted you like I didn't know a man could want a woman. And I thought of homesteading and settling down—and I even thought of kids, too. I still do think of those things, and I still want them—want them with you—or at least a part of me does. A part of me has wanted to stop drifting for a long time now."

"I'm not sure I understand, Casey—part of you

wants me, wants to marry me? What does the other part want?"

I walked to the window and looked outside. "Have you ever seen a big remuda of saddle horses strung out, Lillie—maybe headed back to the home ranch in the fall. They're all tired and walkin' slow, and the cowboys are all tired and sort of draggin' too—and all of 'em, horses and cowboys, are followin' the chuck wagon in. The cowboys don't have much to say because they're thinkin' about the home they don't have—either the home they left behind or the one they've never had. They're tired of their bedrolls and they're tired of the dust and they're tired of cattle that can run thirty miles between waterin's and can bail off a twenty-foot rimrock or hide behind a soapweed. And they're tired of horses that pitch when they're cold and sull up when they're hot.

"And those cowboys'll be thinkin' to themselves as they're draggin' in to the home ranch in the fall that they're not gettin' anywhere and they don't have anything to show for all the years they've followed the different wagons and the different remudas, and they tell themselves that they must be fools to do it and they swear they're gonna stop and get 'em that home on a corner lot in town and get a town job with regular hours.

"But . . ." I looked into the distance and shook my head. "But come spring and green grass, *something* has changed about those same cowboys and those same horses, Lillie. None of 'em are draggin' now! And those same horses that were tired and wore out last fall are now snorty and broncy. They pitch when the cowboys first untrack 'em, but the cowboys are ready for it, and when they cover one with a good ride they can't help but smile and step even a little higher when they get back to earth. And now, cowboys and snorty horses both are lookin' forward to jumpin' a bunch of old mosshorn herd quitters, and tryin' to beat 'em to the rimrocks and tie 'em down out on the flats. And have you ever seen . . . God, listen to me, Lillie. I must sound—"

"You sound like a man in love, Casey," Lillie said with a tear in her eye. "A man in love with horses and cattle and rimrocks and wide open spaces—and freedom. I know you love me, Casey, and I think I know how badly you want me . . . but we won't be leaving here together, Casey. You've got to leave with Johnnie and Ab, and I've got to go—"

"Where?" I asked. "Home?"

"Home?" Lillie said the word softly. "I don't know. That would be wonderful . . . but I don't know if I can."

"Of course you can, Lillie!" I told her. "You can go home, and with your head held high. You've slain all your dragons—and your spiders."

"What are you talking about?"

I grinned. "Never mind. But you can go home. I *want* you to go home, Lillie. Go home for me."

Lillie thought for a few seconds, biting her lip as she mulled it over in her mind. Then her eyes lit up, and she said in an excited voice, "Yes, I can go home! I *am* going home, Casey!"

"The stage will be here any time now! Here . . . take this money that Stagg gave me and Josh. Please. It might not get you all the way home, but it'll sure help—and it's the best use I can think of for it, some kind of justice in it, seems like."

"Oh, Casey," Lillie said softly, with a tear still in her eye. "I don't know how to tell you what you've meant to me—what you'll always mean to me."

"I've never, *ever* known a woman like you, Lillie, and I never will again. Maybe you'll be a famous actress someday, and I can brag about how I know you."

"And," Lillie said in a sad way, "I'll know that you'll be . . . out there"—she made a big sweeping motion toward the window with her hand—"riding free and proud."

"And lonesome," I added.

Then Lillie came slowly and deliberately across the room to the window where I was standing. When she got there, she turned her face up and we kissed, long and tenderly.

"I wonder how many nights in the years to come," I said softly, "I'll lie awake and think about what it would have been like to've kept house with you."

"We could get a hint, I guess," Lillie said with a bright twinkle in her eye where the tear had been.

"What do you mean?" I asked.

"Well, we have a little time before the stage comes." Then she said softly, "Close the door, Casey."

"Are you . . . sure, Lillie?" I said.

"I'm sure," she whispered.

So, an hour later, Lillie Johnson—my Lillie—boarded the stage to begin her long journey home to a place I couldn't even imagine.

And I, with a couple of my own dragons slain, rode off with Ab and Johnnie into the Big Lonely.

We stopped for a moment beside the little cemetery where Josh was buried.

"Seems like a shame to leave Josh here," Ab said.

"Well," Johnnie said, "if you ask me, it would be an even bigger shame to take him with us, bein' as how he's dead."

"A man's death ain't a thing to joke about, Johnnie," Ab said.

"Well, what in the hell else *can* you do with it?"

"I don't know, but you ought to try bein' more like Casey—see how quiet and reverent he is?"

"Oh hell, Casey ain't bein' quiet because he's reverent. Old Case got his little heart broke, that's all that's wrong with him. Maybe he needs one of Dr. Chaise's Nerve and Brain Pills."

I didn't say anything.

When we reined away from the cemetery, Ab said, "Where we goin'?"

"Hell, Ab, we're gonna go to the best cow outfit in the world, where there's lots of good country filled with wild cattle and lots of good horses to gather 'em on—and where the only rules are if somethin' pitches you spur it and if somethin' runs off you tie it down."

"Where's this place at, Johnnie?" Ab asked.

"Well now, you see, Ab, that's the trick—*nobody* knows where it is. If they did, everybody would be there. But it's out there, and we're just gonna keep ridin' until we find it."

We trotted for a mile or so, each alone with his own thoughts. Then Ab said, "I ain't gonna end up like Josh—punchin' cows till you're old and stove up and still broke and then gettin' buried in some lonesome grave a thousand miles from home."

"So how are you gonna do it different?" Johnnie asked him.

"I'm goin' home and get somethin' of my own and settle down."

"Just when in the hell you gonna do this, Ab?"

Ab thought about it, and then he said, "After the work's all done next fall on that good outfit we're gonna find."

Suddenly Johnnie started singing a song all of us had heard before:

A group of jolly cowboys discussin' plans at ease,
Says one, I'll tell you something, boys, if you'll listen please;
You see me now a puncher and mostly dressed in rags,
But I used to be a wild one and went on great big jags.
Now, I've got a home, boys, a good one you all know,
Although I have not seen it since long, long ago.
But I'm going home, boys, once more to see them all,
Yeah, I'll go back home when the work's all done next fall.
That very evening, this cowboy went on guard.
It was dark and stormin' and rainin' very hard.
The cattle they got frightened and rushed in wild stampede.
The cowboy tried to check them while ridin' at full speed.
Riding in the darkness so loudly did he shout,
Tryin' his best to head them and turn the herd about.
But his saddle horse did stumble and on him did fall . . .

*And he'll not go back home when the work's all
done next fall.*

Johnnie's song had a melancholy effect on even
him, and as we rode along in silence, each alone with
his own thoughts again, a loafer wolf's howl came
drifting down to us from the caprock to the south,
faint and far away, mysterious and forlornful, carrying some age-old but unknown message on it.

The Big Lonely was restless as me and Johnnie and
Ab sat adrift upon it once again.